Fully Average

Elizabeth Diane Adams

This is a work of fiction. Names, characters, businesses, places, events, and incidents are either the products of the author's imagination or used fictitiously. Any resemblance to actual persons, living or dead, or actual events is purely coincidental.

First edition
Published by Luna Bear Press
Paperback ISBN: 979-8-9947582-1-2

Luna Bear
—PRESS—

Cover Illustration & Design by Alexandra Fernandes

For all the women who have kept me sane

Amanda, Courtney, Alexandra, Babe, and my mom, Diane.

Thank you.

Chapter 1: Office Space

Melissa Jolene Bonetti considered herself lucky, despite her constant sense of dread. She was fully average, down to her brown eyes, brown hair, height, and weight. This was not, she would tell herself and others, a put down, but rather a fact. A self-deprecating joke with the punchline of her having a steady, decent paying job and a live-in almost-fiance who she had been with since college, named Jeremy.

She was in her thirties and could feel her internal baby clock ticking, but she knew Jeremy wanted to wait. She blamed that for the dread. As she reluctantly gave in to her chiming wake-up alarm, she reminded herself that it was Friday. Soon she would have forty-eight glorious hours to do whatever she wanted. Maybe she would clean the apartment from top to bottom, read one of the books piling on her bedside table, or most likely listen to murder podcasts while playing games on her phone. None of those options included a windowless cubicle, so it was something to look forward to.

Melissa turned off her alarm and reached over to touch Jeremy's side of the bed. As usual for the last few months, Jeremy had already slipped out for a run. Who picks up running in their thirties, Melissa had once asked. Jeremy had quickly quipped the most cliche lines about heart health and longevity.

"What about your knees?" she had said.

"I do not need my knees to live, but I do need this thing to keep ticking," Jeremy had proclaimed, thumping his chest before rushing out the door.

Rolling herself out of bed, Melissa clumsily pulled on the first business casual outfit draped over a nearby chair that was now more laundry than furniture. After throwing her hair into a braid and eating cold spaghetti leftovers for breakfast, she rushed out the door.

As Melissa drove to work, she daydreamed about grabbing a coffee from any of the stands between her apartment and the office but denied herself because of time. She prided herself on being punctual, but the draw of caffeine tempted her to break her streak. She reminded herself that there was free coffee at work and that she wanted to figure out the payment error she had found the day before. A new copy of the accounting books showed a monthly payment for their EID loan marked as unpaid, even though the main ledger clearly listed it as paid.

She wanted to resolve it quickly because, in her mind, there was a real chance this could lead to a promotion or at least a solid bonus. Today was going to be a good day, with or without coffee. Melissa craved this win, followed by the calm of a cubicle free weekend. Pulling into the parking lot, she noticed her manager Bill Gacy's old beat up yellow Corvette was not there yet.

Good, she thought. This would give her time to put together a report and send an email in case Bill tried to take credit for finding the error. She parked, grabbed her free coffee, said polite hellos to her office acquaintances, and sat down at her desk in a small, poorly lit cubicle.

Melissa's cubicle had only a handful of decorations. Two photos, a peace lily plant, a small painting of a stormy ocean, a word of the day calendar, and a mug holding pens with a cartoon cat gripping a knife that read, "I am small and sensitive, but also fight me." One photo showed teenage Melissa with her mother and her best friend, Sloan. The other was more recent, of Melissa and Sloan hugging in the middle while Sloan's husband Zach hugged Sloan on one side and Jeremy stood on Melissa's side with one arm around her and the other holding the camera.

Melissa looked at the photo and felt the chaos in her mind quiet, if only for a moment. She was lucky. She had Jeremy, Sloan, and her mom. She had a steady, normal life. Despite being raised by an artsy, perpetually single mother and a father better known as a glorified sperm donor, Melissa never felt like anything was missing. She had no desire to meet him, and by all accounts she was only fifty percent sure her mother even remembered who he was. A DNA ancestry test had revealed she was a European mutt with a dash of this and that. The only interesting discoveries were that she had ancestors from the Caucasus region, meaning she was technically Caucasian, and that she was a little Ashkenazi Jewish. She did not really know what to do with that information except hold it in her head.

Seeing that her life, at least now, made sense and was not teetering in midair helped her breathe easier.

Turning on her desktop computer, Melissa immediately opened her research on the discrepancy. The PDF showed outgoing payments, but while the payments appeared to be going out, the account they should have been withdrawn from remained unchanged.

Her landline rang, jolting her attention away from the screen.

"Hello, Evergreen Solutions, Accounting Department," Melissa said, glancing at the caller ID, which read Small Business Administration.

"Good morning. My name is Donna Weaver. I'm calling from the SBA to discuss a discrepancy with payments on your EID loan," Donna said, her voice devoid of emotion except maybe boredom.

Melissa scanned the spreadsheet, searching for lines labeled EID or SBA.

"Hello? Who am I speaking with?" Donna asked.

"Oh, I'm Melissa Bonetti. I'm a junior accountant for Evergreen," Melissa said, opening another file in search of proof of payment.

"Well, Miss Bonetti, I've been trying to contact Bill Gacy for over a month. I was beginning to think he was avoiding me, so I'm glad I reached you." Donna paused, and Melissa finally found the regular SBA EID payments listed in the main accounting file. "We haven't received a payment in nearly six months. If we don't receive payment, we will be forced to-"

"I'm sorry to interrupt, Miss Weaver, but on my end it does look like we've made our regular monthly payments. Perhaps there's an error on your end?" Melissa said, summoning confidence while knowing something was wrong. After all, wasn't that what she had been trying to figure out? The error. The duplicate set of accounting records. She had assumed it would turn out to be a training file or another company's books. Now, listening to Donna, she knew it was far worse.

"The government does not make mistakes when it comes to collections. If there is a billing error, it is on your end. Since you are only a junior accountant, I will assume your supervisor is responsible for oversight. Please inform Bill Gacy that unless he contacts me by the end of today, I will assume Evergreen Solutions has no intention of making further payments and that you are acting in bad faith. He has my number and email from the numerous messages I've sent. Miss Bonetti, I suggest updating your resume. Goodbye."

The line went dead.

White noise filled Melissa's ears. She hung up mechanically and rubbed her eyes and face as her heart pounded and her foot began tapping without rhythm. Her phone buzzed beside her, Sloan's name lighting up the screen. The noise faded slightly. Melissa took two deep breaths and answered.

Sloan Levin could easily be described as strong and level-headed. Her sharp wit had drawn Melissa in, but Sloan's deep kindness was what made her stay. They had met in college while attending a production of Hamlet. Sloan was dating the actor playing Hamlet, and Melissa was getting extra credit for an English class. They had sat next to each other, and by intermission, they both knew they were friends. Hamlet turned out to be Sloan's future husband, Zach Wolfe, though thankfully, he had since retired his codpiece and become a high school theater teacher.

Sloan was currently sitting on the bathroom counter next to her sink, miles away from Evergreen Solutions, but desperate to hear her friend's voice. A butter dish sat beside her, and she picked at the edge of a tile as Melissa answered.

"Hey, can we talk later? Something is weird here. I need to talk to Bill," Melissa said, standing and walking to a window overlooking the parking lot. Bill's yellow Corvette had just pulled into its usual space and the one beside it. He had parked crookedly.

"Sure, sure. Yeah. Call me after work?" Sloan said, glancing at the butter dish.

"Definitely," Melissa replied. "Wish me luck with Bill about the bills."

Melissa hung up and grabbed the papers from the printer, highlighting the EID loan payments and scribbling notes about Donna at the bottom of the page before sliding everything into a file. The hallway to Bill's office was not far from her cubicle, but with the panic bubbling in her chest, it felt like a hike she was neither equipped for nor interested in taking. She stopped at his door, took a breath, and knocked.

"Come in, come in," Bill shouted through the thick wood.

Melissa opened the door and stepped into his cluttered office. She watched as Bill pulled a flask from his pocket and took a swig, spilling some onto his baggy, stained shirt. He looked like he had not been home in days. He laughed at himself and dabbed at the spill with a tissue that disintegrated into lint.

"Go on, take a seat. Casual Friday, blah blah," he said.

"Are you sure? I can come back," Melissa said, wanting desperately not to be in this room with a drunk man who controlled her paycheck.

"Nah, nothing matters. You caught me drinking on the job, after all," Bill said with a laugh. He tossed the tissue over his shoulder. "So what's on your mind, Melly Mel?"

Melissa tried not to show her disgust. Bill was not appealing in any sense, and she could not imagine anyone having once found him attractive enough to marry. He had never been professional, but whatever standards he once held had fully evaporated. She tried once more to escape.

"Is now a good time?"

"Oh yeah," Bill said, in a poor imitation of the Kool Aid Man. He noticed the file in her hands and tilted his head. "What's that?"

8

"I found something strange in the numbers," Melissa said carefully. Maybe it would be smarter to go above him. If Donna was not some elaborate prank, something needed to happen now. She considered walking upstairs to the CEO's office. Surely the man who started Evergreen would want to know why the EID loan was not being paid. Panic washed over her as she wondered what else had not been paid.

She set the file on Bill's desk. He opened it and skimmed.

"It looks like we haven't been paying back the EID loan, but in other files it shows we have been. So something's happening. An error. Or something."

Bill's expression dropped from sloppy cheer into raw horror. He read, reread, and closed the file. Melissa stayed silent as he took another drink and set the flask on the desk, twisting the lid back and forth.

"How did you get access to this?" he asked.

Melissa word vomited about server access, initiative, consolidation, all the things Bill had pushed her to do. Then she told him about Donna Weaver and the SBA claiming they had not received payments. She could not stop herself from adding that Bill had not been in for several days and had not returned Donna's calls.

"I thought this was some weird mistake," she finished. "But it isn't, is it?"

Bill nodded softly, his face shifting from horror to something like relief.

"You're fired."

"Excuse me? What? Why?" Melissa said, louder than she meant to.

"Well, not just you. Everyone's fired. This place is dead. Silently terminal," Bill said, turning to his computer and typing.

For a moment, Melissa could only hear white noise and the click of keys. She rubbed her face and breathed deeply.

"So we haven't been paying the EID loan," she said finally.

Bill startled, as if he had forgotten she was still there.

"Oh, we haven't been paying a lot of things." he said.

Melissa stood so abruptly that her chair skidded backward and knocked over a trash can. Bill stopped typing and squinted at her, his eyes struggling to focus.

"Look, kid, I liked you. Okay, I put up with you because you were a great little worker bee who did all the grunt work I hated and the other juniors hated. Ironically, you're the one who figured out our books were cooked. Over baked. A full on lie, riding the edge of criminal before disaster."

He sighed and shook his flask.

"The company is going under in a big way. I'm probably going to jail, because I'm sure the CEO will claim it was my call and that he knew nothing."

Bill smiled to himself.

"But you know what? Screw that. I'm dragging them down with me. I will happily squeal to the police and anyone else who wants to listen."

"So there's no way to fix this?" Melissa asked.

Bill clicked his mouse. The sent email swoosh echoed in the room.

"What are you doing?"

"I already told you. I'm squealing." Bill said, standing and grabbing his things as he pushed past her. "I recommend stealing whatever office supplies you want. Call it severance."

He left.

Melissa stayed frozen until her phone buzzed with a new email. She opened it reflexively.

From: BillG@EvergreenSolutions.com
To: AllCompany@EvergreenSolutions.com
Subject: Effective Immediately You're Fired

All Company,

Effective immediately, all employees are terminated. The company has no money and is moments from being officially fraudulent. Thank Donna from the SBA for hammering the final nail into this coffin. Please direct complaints to the CEO, as I have only followed his instructions. That's right, screw you Craig, I'm not going down for your nonsense.

There will be no return, no comeback, and no severance, as there is no money to serve. Good luck. We're all going to need it.

Go Sox!
Bill

Melissa walked numbly back to her desk. For the briefest moment, there was silence. She sat and steadied herself.

Then the office erupted.

Shrieks, swearing, and raised voices ricocheted across the floor. One voice boomed louder than the rest. Phil from payroll shouted, "Where the hell is Bill?"

"He's on his way to his car." Melissa shouted back. "If you hurry, you might catch him."

Phil was sick of being mocked for being a nerdy numbers guy, so he had responded with a gym membership and a steroid habit. Melissa heard his heavy footsteps thunder past and walked to the window overlooking Bill's parking spot.

Bill had just reached his car, slowed by his drunkenness. Phil caught up to him, calling his name. Bill stumbled as he turned, and ironically Phil had to steady him before he fell. A brief exchange followed, Phil pointing at his phone. Whatever was said ended with a punch.

Bill went down into a patch of decorative shrubs and did not move. Honestly, it was probably for the best. There was no chance he could have driven safely anyway. Phil's rage burned out as quickly as it had ignited, and he turned and walked calmly back inside.

As if this were a signal, Melissa grabbed a banker box from the supply closet, tossing in some sticky notes and a legal pad on her way back to her desk. She packed her belongings while the office dismantled itself around her. The noise faded behind her as she walked to her car.

Across town, Sloan's internal chaos was matching the external collapse at Evergreen Solutions.

She still sat on her bathroom counter, chewing at the corner of a fingernail while feeling like she wanted to crawl out of her own skin. The habit gave her momentary comfort, though she knew she would berate herself for it later. She stared at the garbage can beneath her sink. Inside were two empty pregnancy test boxes.

She glanced at the butter dish.

"Don't be a coward," she told herself. "If this one matches the other, then you'll tell Zach."

She reached for the lid just as her phone rang. Melissa's face filled the screen. Relieved for a valid excuse to delay, Sloan answered.

It took only seconds for her to realize Melissa was not okay, and her own problems evaporated.

"Everyone's been fired. I was fired. I watched Bill get knocked out into some bushes by Roid Boy Phil," Melissa said, skipping pleasantries entirely.

Sloan made a small grunt of shock.

"I'll forward the email," Melissa continued. "Bill was so drunk I'm pretty sure his sweat counted as a cocktail."

Melissa swerved slightly as she forwarded it. Sloan read in silence while Melissa spiraled. She imagined Jeremy's disappointment, his already cautious stance on marriage and babies tipping permanently into no. Her mother's gentle hugs and kind words somehow making the sting worse. Sloan calmly explaining how she might be legally liable.

This was the end of everything. If she had not said anything, maybe Bill could have held the company together for months. Maybe years. Maybe someone else would have figured it out differently. Sloan's voice cut through her thoughts.

"Go Sox?"

"I think it's his auto sign off. He likes sports, I guess," Melissa said weakly. "Is this even legal? Are we even going to get paid?"

"Well, it's not ethical, but if they don't have the money, they don't have the money. You'll need to contact the WEPP. I can help you"

"I can't right now," Melissa interrupted as she pulled into her parking spot. "I just can't handle anything big. I'm going upstairs and making Jeremy hold me or something. I love you. I'll call you later."

The call ended with a soft double beep in Sloan's ear. As if released by it, she opened the butter dish.

On the tiny screen of the test, a plus sign glowed.

Sloan let out a slow breath. Then, the smallest smile crept across her face.

Chapter 2: He's Just Not That Into You

Melissa carried her box from the car into her apartment, defeat echoing in every step. Anxiety churned in her gut as she fumbled for her keys while balancing the box on her hip. When she pushed open the door, she was instantly greeted by the sound of a blender.

Jeremy stood in the kitchen wearing only boxers, his dark hair still damp from a post workout shower. He must not have heard her come in, or her dropping the box on the floor over the blender noise. She watched him for a moment and in that moment, she felt like trash.

How could this handsome, charismatic, fit man ever want a frump like her? He had fixed himself when he started to feel like he was no longer the best version of himself. He took up running, started using minoxidil and finasteride to thicken his hair, and followed Chris Pratt's diet plan. Granted, his jokes, much like Pratt's, had lost some charm, but overall he said he had never felt better.

The blender stopped and he picked up one of the two glasses sitting nearby.

"Hey," Melissa managed. She was still trying to figure out how to tell Jeremy that he was now the sole income for their home. Nauseated, she tried to form the words to explain what had happened. Surprise flashed across his face, but he recovered as he finished pouring the smoothie. Melissa desperately wanted him to pull her into a comforting hug. Jeremy could be incredibly soothing when he wanted to be.

Taking a breath, she blurted, "I'm so happy to see you."

"Hey babe, what are you doing home so early?" Jeremy said, tossing more spinach into the blender.

"Oh, you would not believe the day I've had. Bill lost his mind, the company is in shambles, and I was fired," Melissa began, but her sentence shattered as a beautiful younger woman walked into the room wearing only a towel.

She was so at ease that it suddenly felt like Melissa was the one who had wandered into the wrong apartment.

Melissa forced her gaze to Jeremy, who looked uncomfortable but continued his smooth, practiced motions.

"Who is this?" Melissa said, pointing at the nearly naked woman. Her fragile mental state teetered on the edge of collapse.

Jeremy was obviously having a fling, something meaningless. How was she supposed to forgive him for this? But how could she not? They had been together since college. Eight years of ups and downs. How could she throw away nearly a decade? She would have to punish Jeremy somehow. Maybe this was the catalyst they needed for couples counseling. Maybe this was the event that would bring them closer.

Or maybe she would murder this tiny blonde woman. Jeremy would have to help hide the body. They would be forever bonded by their dark secret. Maybe that was enough. Maybe they would become the subject of a podcast.

Melissa studied the girl again. She looked barely out of her teens. Her stomach dropped.

Was Jeremy a predator? Was this girl still in high school? For the love of everything holy, maybe she would have to kill Jeremy too. At least she would still be podcast worthy. Or maybe they would kill her. She was the obstacle, after all.

"Shit, Mel, it's not what you think," Jeremy started, but a memory surfaced. The girl reminded her of burnt espresso. Melissa lifted her hand and Jeremy stopped.

She turned to the girl.

"Are you the barista who keeps burning my coffee?" Melissa asked.

The girl looked annoyed.

"I have a name, and maybe I would not burn your coffee if you treated me like a human," she snapped. Her voice reminded Melissa of someone throwing a tantrum. "My name is"

"You're in my apartment, naked, with my boyfriend," Melissa interrupted. "I have other questions. Like why are you using my towel. Is this actually my life right now. Your name is not even in my top ten most urgent answers. Do you really think me not knowing your name explains your behavior. Get out."

Rage surged, and she thought again that murder might be reasonable. "How old are you?"

"Babe," Jeremy said.

"To whom are you referring?" Melissa asked calmly, her voice detached from her body. Jeremy blinked, confused, so she continued. "You are screwing her and screwing me over at the same time. So who exactly is babe in this room. Me or-"

She gestured toward the girl, who looked momentarily stunned.

For a fleeting moment, Melissa felt pity. This girl was barely an adult. Jeremy was the adult. Jeremy was the one who cheated. Whether this girl knew or not, he knew.

"My name is Paige and I'm twenty," the girl said. "And actually, Jeremy, I would also like to know the answer to that."

Paige sat in a chair facing him, arms and legs crossed.

Melissa looked at her, rage surging again. A brief thought about Paige's wet towel imprinting the chair crossed her mind. How much of the furniture had ghost imprints from Jeremy and his hookups. She bit the inside of her cheek and forced herself back into the moment.

"You both know I'm just a guy," Jeremy said. "Look, Melissa, I honestly thought I needed to sleep around a bit. We've been together forever. It felt like this stale death march. So I figured if I fooled around, nothing serious, I could get it out of my system and recommit to you. I did this for us."

He locked eyes with her, desperate for understanding. Her rage did not soften.

"I loved you so much, Mel, I didn't even care that you gained a little weight, really. But then I met Paige."

He moved and sat beside Paige, slipping an arm around her. Paige held out her hand.

"I'm Paige," she said.

Melissa shook it automatically, then immediately considered cutting her hand off later.

"Jer Bear is the worst," Paige said. "He obviously put off this introduction for way too long."

She leaned comfortably into Jeremy. They looked natural together, easy in a way Melissa and Jeremy had not been in a long time. Melissa hated admitting it. She shoved the sadness away, saving it for later, alone, in a dark room with blankets and comfort food.

Paige giggled and sighed. "I can't believe I'm going to have a child with such a forgetful man."

"I just didn't want to be cruel," Jeremy said, kissing her forehead.

White noise filled Melissa's ears.

The child was having a child with the man child while Melissa was losing everything. How could Jeremy think this was anything but cruelty. He was comforting his new fiancée while she stood there. Did eight years earn her nothing. No kindness. No decency.

Jeremy stood and went back to the blender, but Melissa saw what he was doing. He was putting the kitchen island between them. Distance. Finality.

"Excuse me," Melissa said. "You're having a child with the barista. You said you weren't ready for kids."

"With you," Jeremy said, not meeting her eyes.

The words hit harder than she thought possible. She stayed frozen, letting them wash over her.

"I said I wasn't ready for kids with you," he clarified, handing Paige her smoothie.

The white noise continued. Conversation felt dangerous.

"I was going to talk to you about Paige," he added. "I didn't want kids without being married, so I asked her to marry me."

Melissa made a sound that barely qualified as human.

She looked at Paige, expecting rage to rise again, but instead sadness flooded in. Paige's expression softened with shame.

"Maybe I should go," Paige offered.

Jeremy took her hand. "No."

Melissa accepted that Jeremy was done with her, but their lives were tangled together. That was what happened when you built a life with someone for nearly a decade.

"Where am I supposed to go?" Melissa whispered.

Jeremy finally met her eyes, and what she saw there was pity. She wondered how long his love for her had been dead.

"Well, since you lost your job, you obviously can't afford this place alone," he said gently. "So Paige and I will take over the lease. Your mom lives nearby. I'm sure she'd take you."

"This is real?" Melissa asked. "This is what you're doing?"

She glanced at Paige, who tucked her hair behind her ear, revealing an oval diamond ring. Melissa's stomach dropped.

It was the ring Jeremy's mother had given him to give her. He had handed it to Melissa years ago without proposing, without commitment, but she had taken it as something meaningful anyway. A piece of his family. A promise adjacent to a promise.

"I'm guessing that's the same ring you gave me," Melissa said. "The one you were getting resized."

Paige glanced at her hand, annoyance flickering.

"The ring was always going to go to the person I wanted to marry," Jeremy said. "I told you, I asked Paige to marry me."

"Go to hell," Melissa said, her anger roaring back. That ring had been hers. His mother would never have approved of it going to a twenty year old barista. That ring had been smuggled out of the old country sewn into his grandmother's coat, according to family legend. This was theft, plain and simple.

"I think you should leave," Jeremy said. "I don't want to be spoken to that way in my home."

Melissa made a strangled noise and turned toward the bedroom. Rage propelled her as she grabbed clothes and shoved them into a bag. Jeremy followed her, insisting this was for the best. His words felt hollow until he finally shouted, "There's no way you were happy. I know I wasn't. You couldn't have been. Were you?"

Melissa froze.

Answering that would break her. Those thoughts were for later. For the dark room. For blankets and silence. She would not give Jeremy her sadness too. He had taken enough.

She grabbed more clothes, her laptop, knickknacks, and her favorite blanket made from old sweaters and shirts. On her way out, she picked up a framed photo of her and Jeremy. It was from their happiest era. Jeremy had one arm around her and the other holding the phone. They were smiling at each other like the world was kind. They had just graduated and moved into this apartment. The joy in the photo made everything feel briefly unreal.

She looked up to see Jeremy standing beside Paige, protective. Paige stared at the floor.

Melissa held up the frame. Jeremy smirked, clearly thinking the same thing she was.

Melissa dropped it.

The glass shattered.

Jeremy's expression shifted from nostalgia to irritation.

Melissa stepped on the broken frame as she walked out with her bags and box. She slammed the door behind her.

"Real mature, Mel," Jeremy shouted.

Across town, in a very different home, Sloan stood in her kitchen wrestling with an oven and a tube of pull apart dough. She was trying to bake rolls. Sloan could dominate takeout menus, but cooking rarely went well.

Her husband, Zach, came home after a long day of listening to high schoolers audition for the school musical. He deeply questioned his life choices. How many times could one hear Defying Gravity, Burn, and Waving Through a Window from Wicked, Hamilton, and Dear Evan Hansen before wanting to quit theater entirely.

He wandered into the kitchen, already sensing pizza in their future.

24

"Whatcha doing?" he asked.

Sloan dropped the baking sheet. The crash was loud. She immediately started crying.

Zach rushed over and hugged her. "Hey. What's wrong?"

"I was trying to do a thing," she said through tears. "So when you got home I could say, guess who's got a bun in the oven. And then you would say something dumb like I don't know or you do"

She bent to pick up dough, and Zach joined her, trying to piece together what she meant.

"Why would you want me to ask about a bun in the ov-" he started, then stopped. "Wait. You're pregnant? We're pregnant?"

Sloan nodded and cried harder.

Zach laughed in disbelief and joy, pulled her into a hug, wiped her cheeks, and kissed her. They had both wanted this. The fear was still there, the same fear as always, but right now they let themselves feel happy.

"I should order pizza, shouldn't I?" Sloan said.

Zach laughed and nodded. "You tell Mel, if she doesn't already know, and I'll order."

Sloan's body stiffened. She wanted to stay in this moment, but she already knew she would answer. Melissa needed her.

"Hello?"

"You would not believe what happened," Melissa said from her car. Her eyes were red and swollen, her face wet with tears. She steadied herself and told Sloan everything. "I left them there. I'm going to my mom's."

"Wow," Sloan said. She had always thought Jeremy was a jerk, but never this kind. "I'll come over tomorrow and we'll talk it through."

"Okay," Melissa said softly and hung up.

She pulled into her mother's driveway.

Chapter 3: Mamma Mia

The outside of the one story beige house had barely changed in the twenty five years since her mom moved her into it in the late nineties. Lavender, rosemary, and sage filled the planter box beneath the large living room window beside the front door. The only recent updates were a new Elect More Women flag waving gently on the flagpole and a gnome holding a light that illuminated the path to the porch. Melissa hated the gnome. She had hated it for nearly a decade, ever since her mom brought it home. Seeing its dumb smiling face now felt like an insult as she watched her mother, Cheryl, swing the door open and hurry toward the car.

Cheryl grabbed the box from Melissa's front seat, every bit the concerned parent trying to do everything she could to help. Her concern was palpable, and the shame Melissa felt at causing her mother pain was yet another layer of hell she had to push through. Melissa grabbed her bag of clothes and followed her mother up the short driveway, which might as well have been a mile long uphill hike for how hard it felt to accomplish.

Once Cheryl set the box down on the kitchen table and closed the door, Melissa let her wrap her arms around her. She sank into the hug, tears flowing freely down her face without sound. Somehow she felt cold, exhausted, and nothing all at the same time, like a void filled with negativity. Cheryl let her cry and waited until Melissa pulled away before saying, "I never liked him. He reminded me of that boyfriend I had when you were about five, Wendell. The whole just being an asshole and now cheating."

Melissa went to her old room robotically. She could not remember if she had responded to her mother or even the drive to the house. Time felt like it was slipping through the cracks of her mind. Her room was still the same as she had left it before college. Books lined floating shelves on every wall. Paramore and Panic! At the Disco posters covered one side. A desk with a mirror sat across from her full sized bed, which was dressed in bedding she would never admit out loud was from Bella Swan's room in Twilight. Melissa knew she was lucky. She had a safe place to land, even if it was an early two thousands time capsule. She had time to figure things out. Still, needing help made her hate herself nearly as much as she now hated Jeremy.

Cheryl leaned against the door frame holding a mug of cocoa. "You need something warm."

Melissa accepted it and took a sip. It tasted amazing and did not even burn her tongue, which somehow felt like a slap in the face. Of all the things that went right today, drinking cocoa felt like a terrible consolation prize. "Thanks, but I think I just need to sleep."

"Unpack a little, drink the cocoa, brush your teeth, and then sleep. You do not need cavities on top of everything else. You will thank yourself," Cheryl said.

Melissa halfheartedly agreed and went through the motions of unpacking, drinking, and brushing. Unsurprisingly,

Cheryl was ready to take the mug and make sure Melissa was in bed. Melissa felt both grateful and resentful.

"You are free to live your best life now that you are done with that job and away from Jeremy. Things will feel brighter in the morning. Good night, baby."

As soon as Cheryl turned off the lights and closed the door, Melissa began quietly weeping again until her mind shut off and she fell into restless sleep. It was not peaceful, but it was better than the waking nightmare she now lived in. She found brief moments of bliss in forgetting, and that was everything. The nothingness she drifted in and out of was the closest thing to relief, and in darker moments, when she remembered who she was in the night, she wondered if that was what death felt like. And darker still, if nothing was the only happiness left for her, would it be easier to disappear into it forever. No shame and no pain. Just nothing.

The first morning waking up in her old room felt like a cruel joke. Remembering she did not even have a job to distract her was another. Realizing her mother was making breakfast and would want to talk was more than she could bear. Maybe she could stay in bed, not move, not even get up to pee despite how badly she had to go, and just wait her mom out. Surely Cheryl would give up eventually.

She underestimated her mother.

Cheryl barged in carrying a tray of food, a hopeful smile in her heart, and a face full of worry. Melissa conceded immediately, knowing she would lose any argument, and sat up. The tray landed on her lap seconds later. Yogurt with fruit. Avocado toast. Most importantly, coffee.

Melissa remembered her manners and mumbled, "Thank you, Mom."

"You are very welcome. Once you are done, we can make our plan about the apartment," Cheryl said as she opened the shades to let sunlight flood the room, then turned toward the closet. She paused and looked at Melissa with eyes only a worried mother could have. The moment she decided to become a mother, she knew it would feel like living with her heart outside her body. Melissa was her heart, and that bastard Jeremy had stomped on it.

"Mom, I can choose my outfit. Thank you. I will eat and then we can handle that, but can I just have a moment to" Melissa trailed off. To what. Gather her thoughts. Feel better. Exist. She did not know. "I just need a moment. Please."

Cheryl took a breath, crossed the room, gently patted her daughter's head, and smiled. "Of course. Eat though. You need your strength."

Melissa shoved a large bite of toast into her mouth to calm her mother's nerves. Cheryl closed the door behind her. Melissa forced herself to swallow, then drank her coffee. It had cream and sugar, like coffee should. Not like Jeremy and his stupid instant and insistence that coffee should be black. Suddenly she no longer wanted coffee. Had Jeremy ruined that too. What else would she lose because it reminded her of him.

Still, she finished the cup. Today was going to be long, and she needed caffeine. She eyed the food and accepted that she probably needed that too.

Once she had changed and eaten, she went into the kitchen where Cheryl was reading the news on her tablet. Cheryl called Melissa at least once a month to troubleshoot something on it, but she loved being able to read whenever she wanted instead of waiting for unreliable paper delivery. Plus, she liked having a reason to call her daughter. She tried to hide how closely she was watching Melissa as she loaded the dishwasher.

Melissa sat across from her. When she settled into her chair, Cheryl took off her reading glasses. Melissa braced herself, anxious about what her mother had planned but relieved she did not have to make decisions. She could just follow directions, however annoying or daunting they might be.

"Okay, you might not like this, but I called Jeremy," Cheryl said.

Regret washed over Melissa for finishing the breakfast her mom made her. Nausea crept into her throat. She did not have to talk to him, but now he knew her mother was involved. Cheryl saw her reaction immediately.

"He said he and the girl will be out of the apartment today. I hired some college boys to help us pack and carry things down."

32

Melissa nodded. This would make things faster, but once she left that apartment, she would be at worst homeless and at best living with her mom. A millennial cautionary tale.

"Okay," she said. "What are we doing with my stuff?"

"I cleaned out the shed out back. Anything that does not fit in your room or that you do not need can live there. I also got Jeremy to agree to buy you out of the apartment, so you will have some money. You will have time to figure out what is next."

Time. She had lost so much of it on a life that was now dead. Today marked the beginning of the mourning period for the future she thought she would have, for the marriage and kids she believed were inevitable. Jeremy was probably throwing a party with his pregnant child bride while she was alone, jobless, and living with her mother.

"The boys will meet us there in about an hour," Cheryl continued. "So will Sloan."

Sloan. The best friend Melissa could ask for. She hated thinking about Sloan because she remembered, sometime in the middle of the night, that Sloan had wanted to tell her something. Even now, it felt impossible to ask. How could she, when the weight of everything from yesterday still pressed on her chest today.

Cheryl put her reading glasses back on and stared at the tablet, sighing. Normally Melissa would ask what was wrong and be assigned a tech problem to solve. It felt like she was trapped under a weighted blanket. Even offering help to her mother felt impossible. Cheryl sighed again, trying to coax her into action. Finally Melissa stood up and walked away. Maybe an hour or two of wallowing would prepare her for whatever came next.

Cheryl watched her daughter wander off, taking with her any chance of figuring out how to get back to her email app. She never quite understood Melissa's devotion to Jeremy or to boyfriends in general. In her better moments, she wondered if her lack of paternal influence had shaped Melissa's desire for what society called normal. Cheryl had made her own choice long ago. After experiencing the darker sides of fatherly relationships, she decided she did not need them. Like Cher, she believed men were cool, but not necessary.

Cheryl made sure Melissa never went without. She never missed meals or lacked clothes or a roof. There were hard times when Melissa was a baby, but Cheryl refused to let single motherhood mean her daughter had less. If she could not afford fancy vacations or trends, she filled their home with art, music, and love. Melissa never had less. She had different.

Once hormones and classmates entered the picture, Melissa started asking why she did not have a dad. Why she did not have two parents. The truth was that Melissa's father, sperm donor, bio dad, whatever he was called, was what you might call a beautiful accident. He had never planned to be father material, something he admitted when Cheryl told him she was pregnant. He had his issues, but mostly he did not want to slow down his life or commit to a child. He did not want part time parenthood or responsibility of any kind.

He was the human equivalent of a tumbleweed who wanted nothing to do with Melissa. It was his loss, in Cheryl's mind, but she sometimes wondered if Melissa had inherited his genetics for depression and anxiety. She never voiced that fear. She knew it would only intensify Melissa's curiosity about him. Cheryl walked a careful line between respecting his wish to stay uninvolved and protecting her daughter by saying she was not sure who he was. She promised herself that would be the only lie she would ever tell Melissa.

Of course, this meant more than one awkward conversation when Melissa asked questions. Cheryl always tried to be age appropriate, but if Melissa asked outright about sex, Santa, or anything else, she told the truth. Ironically, that honesty was exactly why Melissa believed her when she said she did not know who her father was. Maybe that was the best way to keep a lie. Pile truths on top of it until the original lie could no longer be seen or felt.

Chapter 4: Money Pit

Melissa was in her mom's car, driving to her old apartment. She had committed to being there physically, but mentally she was not even sure where she was. Her mom put on Taylor Swift's newest album, and Melissa was not sure if it was meant to make her feel better or her mother. She listened to the words, and Taylor's lyrics felt too real, but she also did not want to face the quiet. So Melissa stayed silent as her mom hummed along to the music.

When they pulled up to the apartment building, dread streaked through her. What if Jeremy was up there waiting to watch her demise. Or worse, what if Paige was up there to be an intermediary. She pulled herself out of the car and looked at her mom. "Is he up there?"

Cheryl explained that he had promised to be on the other side of town, meeting Paige's parents. Melissa guessed they did not have the luxury of time when it came to meeting the parents. She sent a silent plea to God or the universe or really anyone who would listen that Paige's parents would make him squirm and feel ashamed of being a thirty four year old knocking up a twenty year old. She prayed that his family would always ask about her, and that they would always compare Paige to her and find her lacking. She wished them misery, but was very clear that she did not blame the baby. She felt the baby was the only other innocent victim of Jeremy's philandering.

"Hey ladies," Sloan said, walking up with three cups of coffee. She exchanged coffee and hugs with both women. Soon the college boys Cheryl had hired arrived. Both not so secretly, Cheryl and Sloan oohed and aahed over their attractiveness. Melissa understood that they were attractive, but right now they meant no more to her than man shaped tools to help remove her from her old life.

They made their way up the stairs and into the apartment. Melissa looked around. Jeremy still had not cleaned up the frame or the smoothie mess. She rolled her eyes at this. He never cleaned up anything. She wondered if Paige was ready to become a part time maid or if they would bicker over his inability to help with house chores. Or maybe they would enjoy living in a mess. Cheryl took the guys into the bedroom to direct them and Sloan grabbed a broom.

"No, don't touch that," Melissa said firmly. Sloan looked confused, unsure how to react. "He gets to clean it up. He gets to deal with the damage. And don't touch that blender stuff either."

Sloan nodded knowingly and looked around the apartment. She started grabbing things she knew belonged to Melissa. Most of the art on the walls and pretty much anything decorative was Melissa's. Sloan knew that because Melissa had, on multiple occasions, complained about Jeremy's lack of help decorating the apartment. Sloan kept sneaking peeks at Melissa as she browsed through her now broken home. "If you can't be here, you could wait outside if that's easier."

"No. Nothing is easier. It's just a different type of hard," Melissa said. Sloan nodded. She had had her share of bad breakups prior to Zach, though none after a relationship this long. Sloan tried to imagine how she would feel if Zach had cheated and then left her. She had a feeling his car would find itself in a lake and his body in the trunk, but that could be the hormones talking. Sloan continued taking art off the walls and stacking it next to the couch.

Cheryl enjoyed bossing the boys around. Orchestrating them to box, bag, and lift felt like a weird kink she had never realized she had. She had already sold the bed and was planning to leave the couch, but the bed had been sold to a lovely couple who were coming to pick it up in just under forty minutes. She informed Jeremy that she would leave most of the furniture behind, but in a petty move, she knew that beds were hard to quickly replace. She also knew he probably thought she meant something small, like a couch or table. It was not full revenge for her daughter's pain, but at least it was a lasting inconvenience.

By the time the lovely couple came and went with the bed, the rest of Melissa's belongings were packed. While the college boys helped the couple carry it out, Melissa walked through the apartment one more time, confirming that everyone could leave. She stood in each room, debating what had belonged to her and what had belonged to Jeremy and now, she guessed, Paige. She admitted to herself that without her decorative touches, the apartment was colder and more lifeless. She had made this place a home.

She remembered how happy she and Jeremy had been when they first moved in. The one bedroom, one bath apartment had felt huge. It was the real start of their after school life together. They could not wait to start their jobs and move forward side by side. Jeremy used to talk about how there was no one else who made him feel so loved and seen. He used to praise her, hype her up, and pull her out of her blues. That was what they called her bouts of depression. Her blues.

Melissa wondered when it had shifted. How long had Jeremy hung on before giving up on them as a couple. When had he stopped feeling loved and seen, or when had she stopped seeing him and making him feel loved. When had he stopped praising her, hyping her up. When had her blues become too much for him to handle. Maybe she had driven him into the arms of someone easier, simpler, prettier, younger, and less blue.

A hand gently landed on her shoulder. Melissa shuddered and turned to see Sloan, concern on her face. Maybe that was how everyone would look at her from now on. With concern. "The boys are wondering if there's anything else that needs to be packed."

Melissa swallowed and stopped the tears that were beginning to form. "I want to take all the spoons. Just the spoons. Leave the forks."

Melissa had learned pettiness from her mother, and though they had not shared their plans to inconvenience Jeremy, somehow they both found their own versions. The confusion of having no spoons and not being able to easily find matching replacements would annoy Jeremy enough that he would eventually have to order a whole new set, though he would stubbornly delay doing it. Melissa wondered how Paige would navigate the spoon issue. Would it create a wedge between them. Did it matter.

Melissa could never move past this betrayal. Maybe forgiveness could happen one day, but they could never be a them or us again. She had made that decision when she cried herself to sleep after being called fat and kicked out of her home. Still, that did not stop her from wanting him to realize he had made a mistake. She admitted to herself that this desire was normal for any woman treated the way she had been.

"Spoons are packed. You ready?" Sloan called from the next room. Melissa went into the kitchen living room area and looked around one last time. This was it. This would no longer be her home. This would be Jeremy and Paige's place, the starter home for their family, not hers.

"Let's go," Melissa said as she wrangled the apartment key off her keychain and placed it next to the blender. Cheryl wrapped an arm around her and gently led her out. The door closing behind her felt like that saying about God closing a door and opening a window. Except God forgot to mention the window was on the third floor and there was only asphalt and concrete to break her fall. It was tempting.

When they arrived back at the house, most of the boxes went directly into the shed with the help of the college boys. Cheryl offered to make them sandwiches, but they politely declined, explaining they had another move to run to. Her motherly instincts turned to Melissa and Sloan, and their polite declines were ignored as turkey sandwiches were made anyway. Sloan asked if she could have a second for Zach, and Cheryl happily made another. Melissa knew Sloan would try to pass it off as something she had made.

Zach would use his acting skills and say he believed her, but he would know.

Melissa took her sandwich into her room. She took one bite, left the rest on her desk, and let herself fall asleep, back where things hurt a little less and she did not have to think.

Chapter 5: New Moon

Melissa spent the five months since the breakup doing little more than getting up, taking hot showers, eating when forced, and delivering food through DoorDash. It was mostly just so she had a reason to leave the house. She currently had very few bills because her mother refused to let her chip in, so her cost of living was low. Sleep was still the only thing she seemed to enjoy. Everything else felt like going through the motions of living.

She had learned through the social media grapevine that Jeremy and Paige had become lifestyle influencers on Instagram and TikTok. They posted about the pregnancy, their food, fitness, and everything else in between. Melissa blocked them to avoid seeing something that would cause unnecessary pain or disgust. They were allowed to post it, but it did not mean she wanted to see it. Melissa did not post on social media. She did her best to avoid it altogether, except for watching cute dog and cat videos.

Sloan had hung in for the first few months, stopping by and checking in, but over the last two months she came by less and less until it became text messages only. Melissa did not blame her. Her ability to be a friend had dwindled. She needed more than she was able to give in return. Sloan had a full life and needs, needs that Zach and maybe her sister Brooke could meet. Melissa could not.

Melissa knew the people in her circle were worried about her. She simply did not have answers to give. She did not know when she would be back to normal, or if she would be back at all, or what could make her feel better. Even

Zach, who Melissa figured only put up with her because he loved Sloan, reached out. In her better moments, Melissa realized she was loved and cared for, but the figurative wet blanket of depression made everything harder. She wished she could feel normal or be done with whatever these feelings were. She felt more aligned with a zombie, not quite alive but not dead.

Sloan, meanwhile, was killing it. She could not have been happier. Her pregnancy was healthy and strong, according to her doctor. Zach was going crazy building the crib and showing off the sonogram photos to anyone who would look. He was so pumped about the baby that Sloan constantly wondered how she got to be so lucky. After two years and three miscarriages, Sloan had held back her excitement, wondering if this time would stick. Now, nearing the end of her second trimester and feeling her little kiddo squirm around, she felt a peace and joy that was hard to hide.

Zach made a point of singing to her stomach every night, and Sloan did her best to eat right. She hid her coffee addiction from him. It was bad enough she had to give up wine, soft cheese, medium rare steaks, and a variety of other things. Coffee was hers and the baby's secret, and Zach was better off in the dark, like the roast she preferred. Sloan also relented and allowed Zach to do all the heavy lifting and promised to let him put her shoes on if she could no longer see her feet.

Guilt started to build toward Melissa. Sloan did not know when it would be a good time to tell her. Her happiness was palpable, and Melissa was in pain. Seeing her also became more complicated as her stomach began to show. Melissa had not seemed to notice any weight gain, but strangers had begun asking Sloan when she was due, so she knew it was only a matter of time.

Last week, Sloan decided it was time. She would tell Melissa no matter what, at a girls brunch. She had spoken with her sister and her sister's friend Jenna. They agreed to pretend they did not know and act surprised when she announced it. Hiding the fact that Melissa was the last to know was meant as kindness. Sloan desperately wanted to celebrate with her, but she also did not want to hurt her. So she messaged Melissa about brunch and told Cheryl to make sure she came.

The plan was set, and hopefully their friendship harmony would weave back to normal. They could start shopping for baby stuff, she could tell Melissa the names she liked, and maybe she could convince her to go out and start dating again. Sloan was ready to have her friend back. She sweet talked her way onto the brunch reservation list at the Silver Slapjack, the newest, hottest brunch spot. Sloan hoped this would be enough to guarantee Melissa's appearance. They both loved a good brunch.

In Melissa's mind, she tortured herself with wanting her friend back and wanting brunch, while something in her gut pulled at her to cancel. Her depression brain screamed that it would end horribly and that Sloan did not even really want her there. It was surely a pity date. Still, she knew she owed her friend at least a short visit. She could drink mimosas, get Cheryl off her back about seeing friends, and eat waffles. It was probably the best she could hope for in terms of rejoining society. It did not mean she was happy about it, but happiness seemed to be something Melissa had lost all connection with.

Chapter 6: The Breakfast Club

Sloan woke up to Zach softly singing to the baby under the sheets. He was in the middle of *Giants in the Sky* when she opened her eyes. She could feel the baby wiggling. Zach softly sang out the ending, "There are big tall terrible giants in the skyyyyyyy!"

"Morning to you too," Sloan said, and Zach popped his head out from under the sheets. She smiled sheepishly. He quickly kissed her.

"Morning," Zach said as he got up to brush his teeth. "Are you excited to see Melissa and Brooke?"

"I just hope it goes smoothly and that Jenna doesn't fuck it up," Sloan said as she made her way to the bathroom to pee. Zach pretended to respond while brushing his teeth. He knew better than to give his opinion on the matter. "I know, why would I invite her? Because she's Brooke's Melissa. I can't not invite her."

Zach, still brushing his teeth, made an affirmative noise as Sloan finished peeing. She kissed him on the cheek after washing her hands. "You know how your blind agreement and tooth hygiene turn me on. Wanna fool around?"

Zach spat out the toothpaste, wiggled his eyebrows, and took the opportunity to ravage, with tenderness because of the baby, his wife. Sloan giggled as Zach picked her up and carried her back to bed.

Melissa woke up to the sound of her mom vacuuming the hallway outside her room. She looked at her phone. It was

7:00 a.m., a barely bearable time to be awake. She wondered if staying quiet would make her mom move on. Barely moments after that thought crossed her mind, Cheryl threw open her door.

"For the love of Christ, Mom. Why?"

"Honey, I always start my day with a bit of light cleaning. You know that. You've been here long enough," Cheryl said over the noise of the vacuum. Melissa rolled out of bed as Cheryl turned on the lights. "I would love it if you started pitching in with the cleaning."

"Yeah, sure. Maybe after coffee. Or maybe after my heart isn't currently in the middle of being shattered into a million pieces." Melissa pulled on a shabby robe she had had since high school and turned to leave the small, noisy room.

"That may be a tad dramatic," Cheryl said, continuing to clean. Petulant Melissa let out an indignant grunt. "Honey, I only mean that you're not the first human to have to get over a breakup. I'm not trying to take away that you're in pain or say your feelings aren't valid, but maybe it's time to"

"You just want to point out that I'm not healing fast enough. Eight years. I wasted eight years." Melissa flung open the refrigerator and stared at the contents. Cheryl turned off the vacuum.

"Melissa, you are not going to sass me. Jeremy" Cheryl began, but the refrigerator door slammed shut.

"Do not say his name to me." Melissa knew she overreacted, but she could not back down from it. Cheryl raised an eyebrow and put one hand on her hip, full wrathful mom stance. They locked eyes until Melissa looked down in shame. "Please don't say his name to me. Sorry about slamming the fridge."

Cheryl nodded and dropped her hand. "Jeremy is not he who must not be named. He's a jackass who made mistakes, but you did too."

"I didn't cheat. Voldemort did," Melissa said, turning back toward her room. Cheryl stopped her by gently placing a hand on her shoulder.

"What I mean is, you should have left Jeremy and that job years ago. Neither treated you well. I'm not trying to say you deserved what happened. I just mean you should stop thinking about what was done to you and think about what you'd like to do next," Cheryl said, trying to keep her composure, though her concern was only growing.

Melissa took a deep breath, trying to find the right words to make her mother understand. A loud buzz rang from her phone. A reminder. Brunch at Silver Slapjack today.

"I need to go get ready for the brunch thing," Melissa said, stepping away. Cheryl let her walk off, knowing she was not ready for what she had to say and hoping desperately she would take a step forward.

Melissa changed into her finest brunch attire, a baggy sweater, black tights, and UGG boots. She threw her hair into a messy bun and added her darkest sunglasses to complete the look. She grabbed her bag and quietly crept out the front door, avoiding saying goodbye.

Hopping in her car and driving away, a familiar sense of relief washed over her. In her car, alone, she looked normal. No one could see the shame or failure that seemed to reek off her at her mom's house or around anyone who knew what had happened. Her anonymity brought relief. Soon, though, she would have to brace herself. The drive to Silver Slapjack was only ten minutes.

Sloan arrived early. She wanted to make sure her older sister Brooke and her friend Jenna remembered the game plan. She passionately reminded them that if they ruined her carefully constructed ruse, she would personally shove her foot so far up their asses they would taste leather. Both feigned shock but confirmed they would deliver Meryl Streep level performances.

"It looks like she's here," Brooke said. Brooke and Jenna stood and waved until Melissa waved back. Sloan waved too, but stayed low, using the table as camouflage for her pregnant stomach.

Melissa approached the outdoor table, trying to hide her annoyance that it was outside. She gave side hugs to Brooke and Jenna, confused about why Sloan had not stood to hug her. She tried to shrug off the intrusive thought that Sloan hated her now.

"Oh my God, you guys, look at this table," Melissa said, sitting down. "Where's the waiter? Bottomless mimosas on me, ladies."

"Before we order, I actually wanted to share something pretty big," Sloan began. Melissa was distracted, scanning for their waiter, so Sloan grabbed her hand, grounding her. "I wanted to say this to everyone together. We haven't all been together in a long while and"

For reasons Melissa could not understand, panic surged. Her need to stop the moment from progressing overwhelmed her, so she word vomited, "Why would we need to wait to order drinks to hear your news? Brunch means day drinking. Why else would I be wearing leggings and UGGs if not to day drink, am I right?"

"Oh my God, Mel, shut up," Jenna moaned, already over her, which was mutual. Sloan and Jenna shared a look, forcing Jenna back into supportive mode. "Does this news have anything to do with a new skin regimen? Because you are glowing."

"Yeah, you do look a little oily. I have blotting papers somewhere in my purse." Melissa tried to pull her hand away, but Sloan held tight and looked at her best friend.

"I'm pregnant. It stuck. I'm officially deep into trimester two," Sloan said as she slid her chair back to reveal her baby bump. Melissa made noises of confusion and surprise. Sloan smiled hopefully. "Yeah. I'm going to be a mom."

Nausea and shock flooded Melissa. She looked to Brooke and Jenna for guidance on how to respond. They were already asking the right questions about Zach's reaction, names, and how Sloan was feeling. Brief flashes of Sloan's miscarriages and crying on bathroom floors zoomed through Melissa's mind, followed immediately by Jeremy saying he did not want a baby with her.

"And you want the baby?" Melissa blurted.

The three other women stared at her. Confused. Why could she not just congratulate her. How did she fuck this up. Of course Sloan wanted the baby. She had wanted every pregnancy she lost. Melissa had been on the phone with her for two of the three miscarriages. She had been her rock when Zach had to leave for work. Sloan wanted to lash out, but she could see the anxiety spiral Melissa was trapped in, so she swallowed it and tried to play it off.

"I told you Zach and I started trying over two years ago. So yes, we want the baby."

They all forced laughter at varying degrees of believability. Melissa knew she needed to explain herself. She did not want to become a social pariah. So she tried to smooth things over. "Right. Duh. I know. I was just joking. I'm just surprised because don't you look really pregnant."

"I wanted to announce it now because of what happened before. The doctor gave their seal of approval. So I pulled this together because I was hoping" Sloan continued, but her words began to slip away from Melissa. The noise in her head grew louder. The conversation outside her mind sounded like the Peanuts adults. Mouths moved. People laughed. She absorbed nothing.

She did not want to be in her head. She wanted to be with Sloan. She wanted desperately to feel happy for her, but she could not seem to access it. Why could she not be happy for her.

Melissa clawed her way back to the table mentally, catching fragments about how Sloan was barely showing and how their mom had been the same way. Something about their mom dressing like a globe for Halloween when she was pregnant with Sloan. Then it hit her. They already knew. She was the only one who did not. Sloan must have needed to talk about the fear of miscarrying again, and she had not told Melissa because right now Melissa was not a good friend.

A male voice cut through. "Thank you for being so patient. Can I grab your drink orders?"

"Did you still want a mimosa, Mel? Mel? MEL?" Sloan started softly, then louder, until the noise shut off. Melissa snapped back to the moment, but she knew she had to leave. This whole thing had been orchestrated for her. Jenna and Brooke had known. At best, this was a reenactment of Sloan's real announcement. Melissa did not want a fake moment or the feelings swirling inside her.

She stood abruptly and collided with a well dressed woman holding a takeout bag.

"I'm so sorry," Melissa began, then froze. She knew that face. She had not seen her in almost two decades. Rachel Moore. Her middle school tormentor. The first person who made her question her body, her home life, her entire existence. Nothing had been off limits to Rachel's cruelty.

"Oh wow, you need to look where you're going," Rachel said flatly, clearly not recognizing her.

"Rachel? Rachel Moore?" Melissa stammered. Rachel pushed her designer sunglasses into her blonde hair to examine her more closely. Sloan's eyes widened. Melissa had told her about Rachel Moore.

"Do I know you?" Rachel asked, intrigued but annoyed.

"Holy shit, is this the Rachel Moore?" Sloan blurted. For the first time, Melissa looked away from Rachel. Sloan looked confused, but Jenna and Brooke looked like they had hit the lottery. Rachel Moore was still able to collect followers, Melissa thought distantly, as she nodded.

Bile churned in Melissa's stomach as Rachel studied her. Then recognition flickered across her perfect face.

"Moppy? Oh my God. Moppy. Wow. You look great," Rachel said, with her special brand of pseudo kindness. The smile never reached her eyes, yet you wanted to believe her anyway. Rachel Moore was a Regina George without redemption. She would have worn her burn book as a badge of honor, and if a bus hit her, Melissa suspected the bus would break.

Sloan stood, her movements clumsier with pregnancy, and positioned herself beside Melissa. She could tell Melissa had short circuited. "Her name is Melissa."

"I honestly just remember everyone calling her Moppy. Didn't you ever tell them?" Rachel said smoothly. Brooke and Jenna leaned in, fascinated. "Like a mop. Well, it made more sense back then. I used to do this silly prank where I poured water into her backpack, and it left the floor wet like it had just been mopped."

"That sounds incredibly mean and unsafe," Sloan said flatly. She was the only one outraged. Rachel laughed, and Jenna joined in, though Brooke elbowed her when she saw Sloan's face.

"I don't think it sounds funny at all."

"No, it was a hoot. Remember, Moppy? Everyone laughed about good old Moppy keeping the floors clean," Rachel defended effortlessly, flashing her shark smile. "Anyway, I need to go. Hubby's waiting."

"Bye," Melissa managed. Shame flooded her. She could not stand being near anyone anymore. Through the front window, she watched Rachel unlock a shiny new Mercedes with a key fob and drive away. It felt like cruelty had made her more graceful.

"I'm going to go," Melissa said quietly.

She pulled herself away from the group. She heard Sloan call her name, but she had only moments before tears would spill. Those were not for public consumption. That would only bring more shame, and she could not carry any more today.

Chapter 7: Eighth Grade

It was 2003. Justin Timberlake's *Cry Me a River* had everyone believing Britney had cheated, and Myspace had just launched, becoming the first major social media platform. Britney turned out to be a survivor of many liars, and Myspace is now little more than a blurry memory. But for Melissa, this was the year of Rachel Moore. Puberty was hard on everyone, but not Rachel. Rachel seemed to glide through every classroom and social setting with ease, while Melissa had been smacked in the face with pimples, braces, and unruly frizzy hair.

For some reason, and if you asked Rachel herself she would not have been able to say why, she locked onto Melissa as the perfect target for her adolescent rage. Perhaps what drew them together was Rachel's confidence and lack of empathy and Melissa's lack of self esteem and introversion. Or maybe Rachel just needed someone to bully and Melissa happened to be in the wrong place at the wrong time.

Rachel relished finding new phrases and pranks to pull on Melissa, and Melissa dreaded school with every fiber of her being. The school and its teachers gave little credence to Melissa's attempts to stop the bullying and often ignored the situation outright. Rachel had them wrapped around her finger with beauty and charm. Melissa became conditioned to believe her fate was to be Rachel's punching bag.

That acceptance did not satisfy Rachel's appetite for torment, even though Melissa hoped she would grow bored. Instead, it seemed to inspire her to push harder. Knocking books out of her hands, off her desk, or throwing away her lunch was no longer enough. Giving cruel tips about her acne or weight, or comments about her mother being so gross no man would claim her as a daughter, did not provide the same thrill.

The physical stuff began toward the end of eighth grade. Stepping on the backs of her shoes so she tripped. Slamming her into lockers and walls. Locking Melissa in the boys locker room, which came with the added bonus of a week of detention and rumors that she was a pervert. Rachel was proud of the locker room incident, but she wanted more.

One day, walking behind Melissa to class, Rachel noticed Melissa had not zipped her backpack all the way. There was a perfect gap, dead center. Rachel already had a bottle of water in her hand, and like Ben Franklin with his kite, lightning struck. She began pouring the water into Melissa's bag. Melissa only noticed when Rachel shouted behind her, "Oh my God, did you just pee yourself?"

The crowded hallway turned to stare. Melissa looked down and saw the trail of water. Panic consumed her as she yanked off her backpack to check it. Everything paper, including her favorite book *Goblet of Fire* and all her completed homework, had been destroyed. This was the first time Melissa heard the screaming noise in her head. It roared over the cruel chants. The next thing she knew, she was running home, unable to stay at school another second and desperately trying to make her mind stop.

She did not expect to run into her mom. Cheryl was managing a bridal shop, where she was also allowed to offer alterations on the side. Oddly enough, despite Cheryl's disinterest in marriage, she knew how to sell and sew a dress better than anyone. Now, standing in front of her mom with tears streaming down her face, the truth poured out.

Melissa had never told Cheryl about Rachel Moore. Now she told her everything. She expected her mother to hug her and promise everything would be okay. To tell her she needed to stand up to her bully. A classic after school special response. Cheryl did not. Instead, she handed Melissa a box of tissues and put her in the car. She drove straight back to the school and dragged Melissa to the principal's office, despite her pleas to do anything but this. Cheryl did not wait to be invited in, leaving Melissa with the office manager. Both Melissa and the office manager could hear Cheryl's tirade.

"Do you know who my daughter is, who I am? You really should if you know anything about what's happening in this shithole of a school. My daughter has been tormented for almost a full school year and you and your staff have done nothing. Explain that," Cheryl shouted. There was a pause as the principal tried to explain himself. It did not satisfy Cheryl. "She has been assaulted and your suggestion is having a chat?"

Later that day, Melissa sat in a classroom with her mother, Rachel, Rachel's parents, a handful of teachers, and the principal. Melissa was nauseated the entire time, shame and guilt swirling inside her. The meeting stayed civil until Rachel was asked for her version of events.

"I'm not sure what Melissa has said, but I thought we were friends. I would never do anything to hurt her feelings on purpose. If her feelings were hurt, she should have told me. How can I be sorry for something I didn't do?"

Melissa could not stop the tears streaming down her cheeks. Mr. Moore scoffed. "Oh, here we go. Playing the victim. This is why kids are getting participation trophies."

"Excuse me? You're raising a little sociopath and you're blaming my daughter?" Cheryl replied calmly, daring Mr. Moore to push further. Mrs. Moore, who looked like an older version of her daughter but heavily medicated, remained quiet, just how Mr. Moore liked it.

"You mean future CEO. My girl is bound for greatness. Yours will be lucky if she finds a schmuck to marry her. After all, you couldn't manage it," Mr. Moore spat. That was when the principal stepped between them.

"I think we are getting sidetracked here. Let's take a pause," he said, trying to defuse the tension. Cheryl stood closer to Melissa and farther from the Moores. Melissa felt her mom's hand settle on her shoulder. "We have a case of she said, she said. This is my call. I think what's best is for both girls to agree to keep their distance. Staff will keep an eye out, and if anything inappropriate happens, it will be dealt with appropriately. Can we all agree to those terms?"

"You mean you're doing nothing until something else happens," Cheryl said.

Another hour passed in back and forth. Mr. Moore spewed his opinions. Cheryl did everything in her power not to murder the Moores. The result was the same. Rachel and Melissa were instructed to stay far apart, and in classrooms they would sit on opposite sides. Every teacher swore to Cheryl they would be vigilant, but she knew it was impossible to give special attention to one student out of twenty five.

Shockingly, Melissa had a full week of peace. Being ignored was bliss. Rachel had spread a rumor that Melissa's mom had herpes and that it was passed by touch, so Melissa probably had it too. Everyone stayed away, which was an improvement. Melissa began planning the rest of her public school career. No social life was not ideal, but it was survivable.

Slowly, teachers dropped their guard, distracted by newer problems. Rachel seized the opportunity to resume her torment, but got better at hiding it. The water pouring into Melissa's backpack became so routine that she started packing homework in plastic bags. This was when the nickname Moppy took hold. It went on for weeks, escalating until Rachel's final pour.

Two Fridays later, Rachel was feeling frisky. She spotted Melissa turning toward the stairs to head to history class and poured a full bottle of water into her bag. Rachel did not know how Melissa had missed partly unzipping her backpack, or how she had not felt the dripping turn into streaming water. But just as Rachel was about to shout Moppy, Melissa slipped and tumbled down the stairs.

After an ER visit, Melissa learned she had a sprained ankle, bruises, and a mild concussion. What mattered most was that Rachel had been caught. A teacher saw everything and reported her. Finally, there was proof. True to the school's zero tolerance policy, Rachel Moore was expelled. Suddenly, Melissa's horror story ended. The monster was dead. Never to be heard from again.

Melissa slowly rebuilt her self esteem through therapy and managed to make acquaintances who kept her company until graduation. True friendship came when she met Sloan. Love came when she met Jeremy. Her real life began in college.

Until everything fell apart again, and like a horror movie, the monster rose.

Chapter 8: Little Miss Sunshine

It took Melissa some time to calm down once she was alone in her car. She was beyond grateful that no one had followed her while wondering if she should be sad that no one did. Since she had skipped brunch, she grabbed herself a breakfast sandwich and ate it alone in her car. She could hear her phone buzzing but didn't want to talk to anyone.

As she chewed her egg, sausage, and cheese sandwich, she thought about how Rachel Moore seemed to be living a perfect life. Everything went right for her. But how? Shouldn't she be in jail somewhere? Or living in squalor? Or at least single? Melissa let these thoughts roll around her mind, bouncing back and forth until one conclusion remained. Rachel didn't deserve her life or her good fortune.

Surely a person as rotten as Rachel Moore needed to be exposed as the hell spawn she was. The people in her life must not understand who she really was or what she was capable of. Karma or the universe or whatever had put Melissa in Rachel's path again to help make things right, and maybe by doing that, Melissa's life could be made right too. She started her drive home, where she knew she could dive into research on Rachel Moore.

On the drive back to her house, Sloan berated Jenna for her inability to read a room, that her invite to breakfast had only happened because of Brooke. Brooke did her best to stand up for her friend, but based on the information Sloan had given about Rachel Moore, she had to relent that they had been wrong to fall under her spell. Sloan pulled herself out of the car, flipping Jenna off as the car drove away. Even if they got mad at her about the gesture, pregnancy was the ultimate mic drop of blame it on my hormones, and Sloan planned to use it as often as she could pull it off.

Of all the things Sloan hated, seeing her family hurt was at the top. Melissa had become her sister many times over. Brooke had gotten in because of shared parents, but Melissa had held her hand and hyped her up in the bad times and typically was the first one to celebrate the good times. This reaction from Melissa was new, and Sloan didn't know how to help her friend. Sure, more than once Melissa had fallen into bouts of depression, but this was by far the most severe and longest one Sloan had ever seen her go through.

Zach was flipping through the pages of Heathers the Musical: Teen Edition, the musical his department was able to afford, while lounging on the couch. He looked away from the pages when Sloan walked through the front door. She gave him a look that told him brunch hadn't gone well, and he responded with a look that told her to come cuddle.

As Sloan allowed herself to collapse on top of Zach, he refused to let a grimace escape. Sloan was appropriately sized in Zach's book, and he refused to be the reason she got a complex about her changing body.

"Do you want to talk about it, or do you want me to distract you with the horrors that await me for this musical?"

"You know, it didn't go well, and I probably should have told her sooner, but I couldn't have planned what happened," Sloan began. She continued with the story of what had happened at brunch. "I mean, it was just bad luck. I don't know what's going on in her head right now. I used to feel like we could read each other's minds."

"Oh, that's probably a pregnancy brain thing. You should start resenting the baby for taking away that super friendship power," Zach joked while rubbing her side. Sloan groaned in response. "She needs time to process. She'll reach out when she's ready. And then she'll kick herself for not rallying faster for you."

"I don't want her to kick herself," Sloan said.

"Yeah, but she will," Zach said before kissing the top of her head. "I've watched you two for a while now. I know how much love is there. She'll be mad that she missed this much time. She'll be mad at herself and at the depression."

"I should have told her sooner," Sloan responded.

"And you'll blame yourself. And thus the cycle of girl friendship will be complete," Zach laughed. Sloan not so gently slapped his chest.

"You're not supposed to be that insightful, you're the guy," Sloan said, laughing back at him. Zach shrugged and began reading the script again. Sloan watched him for a second before closing her eyes. In the moments before a nap overtook her, she concluded that she loved Zach with her whole heart, and if he ever pulled something like Jeremy, no one would be able to find his body. No Body, No Crime's melody began to play in her mind, and sleep found her.

Melissa had managed to sneak past her mom and slip into her room. She tore off her clothes for shabbier sweatpants and a hoodie. She pulled her blanket around her, got comfy on her bed, and opened her laptop. Immediately, she ordered a background check and started googling Rachel Moore. Articles about her collegiate golf career, the company she started, an announcement about her wedding, and her socials were all open in tabs on her browser.

Rachel Moore had made a very successful life for herself. Mr. Moore had been right about his daughter's success. Granted, he was dead according to Melissa's research. She compiled all her findings into a file on her desktop labeled Karma. She wasn't sure how this information would lead to revenge, but until a plan was formed, she would collect everything. She even found out that Rachel's husband had taken her last name and that he called himself her trophy husband.

Chapter 9: Life of the Party

A few days later, a ding ding rang out from Melissa's email, alerting her that Rachel Moore's background check was ready to review. Melissa's internet search had revealed very little in terms of actionable information. Rachel had cultivated a life that most people would dream of creating for themselves. There wasn't a single reference to any childhood mishaps, criminal misdoings, or even negative reviews. So as her finger went to double click the report open, Melissa's heart began to race and her breath stilled.

Most of the background check confirmed what she already knew or gave more context. Rachel had no record, her credit score was ranked as excellent, and she had graduated from Columbia University. What was new information was Rachel Moore's home address and that she had more parking tickets than the average person. Infuriated, Melissa shouted, "How in the actual fuck?"

"Swear jar!" Cheryl shouted back, then moments later walked through the door holding a basket of folded laundry, which she immediately began putting away. Melissa barely moved but rolled her eyes.

"Knock, Mom. I could have been naked," Melissa said halfheartedly as she reread the report.

"It's my house, and it's nothing I haven't seen before," Cheryl scoffed. When she finished putting away the clothes, she turned around to examine her daughter. "You need to eat. You're really starting to freak me out with this whole Penn Badgley vibe."

"Ugh, I'm not going to murder anyone, and internet stalking is how my generation processes," Melissa said. She had instantly regretted telling her mom about her research, but she'd needed an ear to vent to about Rachel's perfect life. To Melissa's dismay, her mom had only been mildly interested, chalking it up to sociopaths always succeeding in business.

"Sloan called," Cheryl said, waiting for Melissa to speak. After a long beat of silence, she continued. "She called to tell me that she announced she's pregnant. Why didn't you tell me?"

"I don't want to talk about it," Melissa said. She'd been able to distract herself from the shame of not being by Sloan's side by obsessing over Rachel. Her mom wanting to dissect that was not going to help Melissa with her wants or needs. "You know how you called Jeremy my Voldemort? Well, Rachel is my Umbridge. I need to understand how that living Bratz doll managed to have this amazing life. Didn't you tell me that Karma would take care of her?"

"Oh honey, who said she didn't? She was expelled after the stair thing. We don't know what," Cheryl said. She continued talking, but Melissa tuned her out, not wanting to be discouraged from her path of revenge. That was until Cheryl asked, "Maybe it's time we bring in Dr. David again?"

"I don't need therapy. I'm just a little sad. It's normal. My whole generation is sad. It's our normal," Melissa said, rolling out of her blankets and heading to the bathroom.

She figured if she started grooming, her mom would leave her alone. Cheryl was undeterred, leaning on the door frame of the bathroom.

"I need you to be scarce tonight," Cheryl said with a firm tone. Cheryl had decided that if Melissa was going to be a permanent fixture in her home again, she was going to start taking off the kid gloves. Melissa looked at her mom in confusion as she continued brushing her hair. "Honey, I have a date."

Melissa heard her mom but was suddenly distracted by a blackhead. She gave up on trying to talk her mom out of dating immediately. Rationally, her mother was an adult and allowed to do what she wanted in her home. It didn't mean either one of them wanted the other nearby for that.

Melissa decided to go to Sloan's. It was time to put in some face time with her friend, and her location had other added benefits that she would tell Sloan about in person. Perhaps Sloan would be willing to help her take down Rachel Moore, and then they both could move on. Focus on Sloan's baby and rebuilding her own life. Maybe she could get pregnant without a man. After all, her mom had made the choice to have her and raise her without one. For the first time, Melissa considered the possibility that maybe her mom had gotten it right all along and that she had simply been ahead of her time.

Getting into her car and heading down the familiar path, Melissa began to think about how she and Sloan had met. Agreeing to go see that play alone for extra credit had been maybe the best move she'd ever made. Having Sloan, a real friend, after so many years of isolation and rare peer interaction where she'd been treated as an outcast was like taking her first breath after holding it underwater. It had saved her life. She'd met her platonic soulmate in Sloan.

She knew Sloan had felt similarly. It was different in the sense that Sloan hadn't had a hard time in school. She had naturally been a confident introvert, hence why her extrovert of a husband always seemed confused by her inability to enjoy parties. He socially butterflied his way through so many cast parties, keggers, and now office parties, only to come home, swear he'd never party again, and pass out in the softest pajamas he could find. Melissa couldn't even manage the fake it till you make it approach.

Anxiety had firmly gripped Melissa, never allowing her to feel confident in socializing. It was safer not to try than to face the overwhelming rejection. Sure, she would go to parties with Sloan, that's how she met Jeremy. It was at the Pi Kappa Alpha Spring Freedom Swing Party, which was an excuse for the men to wear kilts without underwear in honor of Scottish tradition, although most of the frat boys participating either weren't actually Scottish or didn't know where Scotland was.

It was the first time she saw a penis in real life, and simultaneously it was also the most penises she'd ever seen on a single night by a very large margin, a record which had stood the test of time. Jeremy was the first guy she met that night who didn't lead literally dick first. He'd made her feel more at ease in the sea of raging penises. Sloan had been taken to the backyard to watch Zach in full theater frat boy mode doing a choreographed dance in his kilt. To preserve their new friendship, Melissa had stayed inside.

So as EDM music spliced with bagpipes rang throughout the frat house, Jeremy wooed Melissa. He talked about his big plans and how he was really close to his parents. As he talked about himself, Melissa felt like she was able to check off an imaginary list for a dream guy that even she hadn't realized she had. Finally, she remembered when he whispered his big secret of the night. Jeremy had sneakily worn underwear with his kilt, cheating the only actual rule of the party. At the time, Melissa felt like he was including her in on his innocent rebellion.

She pulled up to Sloan's house when a realization occurred to her. Maybe Jeremy had always been a cheater at heart. Sure, it was only the act of wearing underwear, but he also could not have come or just worn pants. Melissa asked herself how she hadn't made that connection once in the last five months of dealing with the breakup.

Suddenly startled, she turned her head toward a knocking noise. Sloan started waving at her through the car window. Melissa managed to smile back as she turned her car off.

Chapter 10: Bombshell

Sloan's home was warm and inviting, just as she and Zach made it. It was horrible in the way that seeing stable love felt like for someone like Melissa. She hadn't come over since before Jeremy, and she hadn't realized that maybe she had unconsciously avoided it. Sloan had a bottle of grape juice and a bottle of wine chilling on the table with two wine glasses and string cheese. Melissa looked at her friend, hoping desperately that she couldn't see the pain that her happiness caused her because she was also happy that Sloan had everything she wanted.

"Best I could do on short notice," Sloan said with a scrunched up face. Sloan loved a good charcuterie board, but in her condition soft cheeses, cured meats, and wine were not on her list of approved pregnancy foods. "I can send Zach to go pick us up food or something if there's something"

"Shut your beautiful face, this is perfect. Please don't take this the wrong way but your stomach is huge," Melissa said, trying to see if their friendship could begin again at its normal levels. Sloan immediately turned to the side, stuck out her stomach, and rubbed it.

"I'm more than huge, I'm massive. It looks like I stuffed a poorly inflated beach ball up my shirt. Oh shit, do you want to feel it kick?" Sloan asked, but didn't wait, grabbing Melissa's hand and shoving it onto the spot where the kick could be felt. Melissa started tearing up, overcome with joy for Sloan and also, surprisingly to her, she was so excited to meet this little human. Sloan caught her eye and they began to laugh together. "I'm glad your mom has an active sex life."

They both laughed even harder until they were forced to sit on the couch.

"What possessed you to say that?"

"Well, one, it gives me hope that I'll still want to bone when I'm her age. And two, I don't know if you would have left your hidey hole without the threat of hearing your mom's sex sounds," Sloan admitted. Melissa's smile dropped into a more thoughtful expression. She knew Sloan had clocked her disappearing act, but wasn't sure what to say or how to explain.

"You want to tell me why you never told me about the Moppy nickname?"

"I don't know. We met in college and I didn't want to risk that nickname following me. Because it wasn't relevant anymore?" Melissa said as she hugged a couch pillow. Sloan poured her a glass of wine and herself a glass of grape juice.

"Okay, well, obviously it is," Sloan said as she handed Melissa the wine.

"I just always thought that in my mind, Rachel was punished via Karma. Those people who suck get their just desserts. If anything, it seems like her life just got better and better," Melissa said, but she could see that Sloan wasn't on board. She pulled out her laptop quickly, showing her the most damning article proving her point called Picture Perfect Girl Boss: Rachel Moore. "Look at this. She's being promoted like royalty. There's not one mention of a regretful past or seeking redemption. She's thriving."

Sloan took the laptop and read the article. It was overly kind, no hardballs, no real point. Sloan concluded this was a filler puff piece that may have even been paid for. However, when she exited out of the one article and found over two dozen more articles Melissa had saved, she looked back to her friend and said, "Jesus, Mel, this is a little bit of a lot."

"I had to know. I did all the things. I was nice, I got the degree, the steady job, and the guy who loved me more than I loved him. I did everything right," Melissa said, her thoughts coming out unable to be stopped.

"Whoa. You thought Jeremy loved you more than you loved him?" Sloan blurted out, holding Melissa's hand. "I don't mean this to sound wrong, but what makes you think that?"

"That's what he used to tell me all the time. That there was no way I ever loved him as much as he loved me. Which I thought was supposed to be what you wanted and I did until" Melissa tried to remember the moment, if it had been before the barista, if she'd seen something or suspected something, but she didn't. She really did believe him. "Yeah, until I came home after being laid off to find him with that barista who used my towel to shower with."

"I still don't go to that cafe in solidarity." They both gave each other weak smiles. Both knew that the only reason either of them went there was because it was so close to her apartment. To go there now would be to make a special trip, so it wasn't a big loss. Melissa did appreciate the confirmation from Sloan though. Sloan put a comforting arm around her as Melissa pulled the laptop back open.

"Did you really pay for a background check?"

"I mean it was like twenty dollars, it's fine. I just wanted to see if she had a criminal past or high debt. I thought that maybe it would be something really obvious, straightforward, that could take her down," Melissa said as she watched Sloan scan the document. She was waiting for Sloan to realize the same thing she'd made out about Rachel Moore's address.

"Holy shit, she lives like a few blocks away," Sloan said, mapping out her neighborhood in her mind.

"Really? I didn't realize," Melissa said, as a Cheshire smile crossed her face. Sloan hit her with a pillow, both laughing.

"You know. That's why you came over," Sloan said as she rolled her eyes. After a moment passed, she stood up and started putting on shoes. "Okay, let's go then. Let's see the monster's lair."

Melissa gleefully got up and pulled her shoes on. She was so happy to have her friend back. It made trying to remember why she didn't reach out sooner almost impossible. Sloan led the way, as she knew the neighborhood layout well. She'd done a lot of research when she'd bought the house, taking it as a challenge to get the best deal possible for herself and Zach.

Just a little over two blocks away was Rachel Moore's McMansion. Her pretentious house dripped in suburban status quo, from its oversized garage, multiple stories, and bay windows. Melissa stood across the street pretending to read a flier with Sloan about a kid who was willing to mow lawns for cash, as she took in Rachel's home. Her stomach began to ache, and the white noise returned, but softly, making the world seem more distant.

"What the hell, right? What's Karma even doing?" Melissa said softly, pretending to point at another poster for the block party. "How much do you think that house is worth?"

"Well, I don't know because I have no idea when she bought that," Sloan responded, but then Melissa gave her a look. "Ugh, okay, its value today is probably five million. Maybe five point five. It really just depends on so many factors."

Sloan continued on, explaining the factors to Melissa, but besides the occasional "yep" and "I know, right," she wasn't participating in the conversation. Melissa stood there, allowing her brain to launch into overthinking the question, How do I get revenge on someone who has the perfect life? With no flaws or defects to exploit, what could take her down? Sloan began to notice how checked out Melissa was.

"So what, she has money, she owns that house, has her own business, and has a loving husband. You know how they say if something looks perfect, it usually isn't? There's no way that her life is perfect," Sloan said, trying to soothe Melissa, which worked.

"Fingers crossed for a failing foundation," Melissa said, a thought of a plan beginning to form. "I just need to find out how her life isn't perfect."

"I just mean, you're seeing what's accessible online. People don't post the bad stuff. I guarantee you, there is some Gone Girl bullshitery going on in there. Mark my words." Sloan turned to leave, but Melissa paused, no longer pretending to read fliers and just staring at the house.

"Why? You didn't even talk about her for years. When's the last time you really even thought about her?"

"I don't know. But since bumping into her it feels like 2002 again and I'm twelve years old. So my brain won't shut up about her," Melissa said quickly, hating to admit her weakness with Rachel Moore, but another thought popped into her mind. "Did you know that she claimed to be related to Mandy Moore? Like from Princess Diaries."

"And I'm related to Anne Hathaway," Sloan said, letting her sarcasm shine.

"In the right light, you can see a resemblance," Melissa relented.

"Hey Mel. Mel," Sloan said, trying to break through the spell Rachel Moore's house seemed to have over Melissa. She blinked heavily and then looked at Sloan. "Okay, then what do you need to get to move on from this because you need to get your shit together. I need you to get your shit together."

"Why? I'm really hitting my stride with being a mess," Melissa tried to joke, hoping Sloan would take the bait to move on, but no such luck for Melissa.

"Well, I'd prefer the godmother of my child not to seem like a prequel to Fatal Attraction," Sloan tried to be casual, but Melissa realized the weight of that revelation. "I thought about making it Brooke, but she used to fart on my head while we grew up. Not even over my dead body would I let Jenna. She is Jenna after all. So yeah, you."

Another rush of gratitude washed over Melissa. Linking arms, they began to walk back to Sloan's house together. Melissa knew at that moment that Sloan was right. She couldn't and shouldn't be a mess forever, but how much time did Melissa have to embrace her Karma crusade against Rachel?

"You got four months before this nugget comes," Sloan said, patting her stomach gently.

"I think I can work with that. How together are we talking?" Melissa asked. Four months should be enough time to find some way to destroy Rachel, but would it be enough time to do that and pull her shambled life together? She wasn't sure.

"Somewhere between a Miley Cyrus post Liam Hemsworth and Grammy win. Like, you don't have to have the Grammy but progressing toward it," Sloan said thoughtfully. "Currently, you're giving a Bangerz era. There are bops but at what cost?"

"Ouch. Words hurt, you know," Melissa said, pretending her heart hurt from the verbal bashing. Sloan chuckled, but her face drew back to seriousness quickly.

"I love you and hear you. I'll be somewhere between that in four months."

Melissa said the words and wanted to believe them as much as Sloan did, but she had a lot to do and not a lot of time to accomplish it. She needed to focus. She needed the information that could only be found inside Rachel Moore's house.

So she was going to have to commit a crime. She was going to have to do a B and E. First, she'd need supplies.

Chapter 11: Trainwreck

Leaving Sloan to go back on her mission of destroying Rachel Moore felt like a double edged sword. On one hand, she didn't want to leave, enjoying the comfort their friendship gave her. On the other, the draw of finally putting Rachel in her place was too tempting to ignore. She instinctively drove to the cheapest big box retailer she could find.

Hopping out of her car, she walked into the back of the store where the camping gear was. A store employee approached her with a friendly, "Is there anything I can help you with, sir?"

She didn't stick around to find out if the comment was intentional as the employee immediately walked away. Melissa vowed never to come back to this store. She took the sir as a direct insult and turned around, leaving to go to the next available option, a local store people went to when they wanted to shop local, called Stone's Throw Grocery and Homegoods. Their slogan was It's just a stone's throw away.

Melissa got out of her car again, slipped into the store, and headed to their sports and camping section. She picked through supplies, trying to think about what she would need. She started to feel uncomfortable lingering in the hunting area with bows and ammo. The night vision goggles caught her eye. Little did she know, a Stone's clerk named Logan was walking toward her.

Logan was tall, with short auburn curly hair, blue eyes, and a smile that could put anyone at ease. Sure, he'd been miserable with boredom five minutes earlier, but Melissa had caught his eye. He noticed how she'd made a quick beeline to the camping section despite her general demeanor suggesting she'd never want to be in the woods hunting. For a moment, he wondered if she was a disgruntled woman on the verge of murderous intent and if he would eventually appear on the local news as the clerk who sold her the weapon used in the crime. But as she avoided anything weaponlike, his curiosity only grew. Finally, he decided he had to know what her deal was and made his way over.

"Planning on doing some night hunting?" Logan asked when he saw the box in her hand.

"Oh, no. I don't like guns," Melissa said, already trying to build walls against this clerk.

Logan wasn't easily deterred. He wanted to satisfy his curiosity.

"Alright. Then may I ask what you plan on using them for? Because I'm starting to worry you might be a serial killer," Logan said, trying to joke.

Melissa didn't want another sir incident and took too long to respond, so Logan continued. "Night vision goggles are usually used at night. So I assume you have night plans."

"I'm planning... I'm doing recon," Melissa said, trying to find the right words.

Logan remained unconvinced but stood there with a carefree smile. He liked this woman, whoever she was. Melissa set the box down.

"I'm a private investigator."

"Bet? Have you ever caught a criminal on the run?" Logan asked. He knew she was lying, but she was killing the monotony of his day and he wanted to stay as long as possible.

Melissa had the opposite goal. She wanted supplies and silence. She hoped for self checkout, but she needed help.

"I think you're thinking of a bounty hunter. I'm new to being a PI, so I'm still getting set up gear wise," Melissa said. She tried to think of a fake case but all she could think about was what happened to her. "I was hired to catch a husband cheating. The wife thinks he's sleeping with a twenty year old barista. It's my first catch a cheater case."

"Damn, infidelity is lame ASF," Logan said thoughtfully. The way she said it made him wonder if she was really looking for herself. If that was the case and she wasn't trying to murder anyone, he felt like helping was a good deed. "Well, those goggles can't take photos, so they wouldn't give you proof. Plus, they can't see through curtains or blinds."

"Can something see through curtains?" Melissa asked, unable to hide her excitement.

"Not really. I think you just need a camera. Maybe like some bugs and tracking devices," Logan said, trying to think what he'd use. "We don't sell those here, but I bet you can get them on Amazon."

Logan was surprised by the feeling in his stomach as he watched Melissa leave the store. He suddenly wished they carried spy gear, but he doubted lightning like her would strike twice. He forced himself back to the register and the monotony of the night, but kept thinking about her and what she was really up to.

Melissa was already in the parking lot, shopping on her phone. An all-black outfit, black backpack, camera, lockpick kit, listening devices, and tracking devices all went into her cart. She hesitated for a moment, debating whether this was really what she should do, but before reason could win, she pressed purchase. The items would be on her mom's doorstep in less than twenty-four hours, and Melissa could continue her plan.

Having decided on a classic breaking and entering, Melissa would plant listening devices and take photos of everything. She would find whatever secrets Rachel Moore was keeping and ruin her with them. The breaking and entering part seemed hardest but totally possible. A few lockpicking videos could teach her how to use the kit, or maybe she'd find an unlocked window and simply roll on in.

When Melissa got home, she crept to her room, plugging her ears. Thankfully, she didn't hear sex noises from her mom's room. Either the date hadn't gone well or they'd already finished. Whatever the outcome, she was relieved not to be even peripherally involved. She changed into soft pajamas and collapsed onto her bed. For the first time since before her life imploded, Melissa drifted into a peaceful, dreamless sleep.

The following morning, Melissa lay in bed watching YouTube videos about lockpicking. She'd been watching and taking notes for an hour and still didn't feel confident. A knock at her door broke her concentration.

"Honey, you got a package!" Cheryl said through the door. Melissa rolled out of bed and threw it open.

"See, I knocked."

"Yes, thank you, next day shipping!" Melissa said, holding up the box as she walked back to her room.

"I haven't seen you this excited about something in a while. What did you get?" Cheryl asked, smiling at her daughter's energy.

Melissa knew telling her mom the truth would only lead to attempts to stop her, which wasn't an option. A half truth would have to do.

"It's nothing. Just a new hobby... photography," Melissa said, trying to get past her.

"You know your Auntie Claire does photography too," Cheryl said, trying to connect.

Melissa shrugged and slipped past her. Cheryl sighed but gave her space, hopeful photography might help pull Melissa out of her depression.

Alone in her room, Melissa unboxed her gear. She felt bad lying, even halfway, but she also knew the healthier option would be abandoning the plan and calling Dr. David again, which would mean never getting justice for her middle school self.

She pulled up an article where Rachel talked about keeping her marriage passionate through Saturday night date nights. Melissa figured that meant every Saturday night would be her window. She had a few days to learn the camera, install bugs, and pick locks before then.

Finally, Melissa felt busy again. Purposeful. Like taking a breath after holding it underwater just to see how long you can last.

Chapter 12: Date Night

Arriving at Rachel's house that Saturday night felt both thrilling and terrifying. Melissa sat in her car listening to Paramore, trying to stay pumped and drown out any thoughts of backing out. Since she didn't know when or if they would leave, she parked close enough to see the house but far enough back that Rachel wouldn't recognize her.

After a few hours of waiting, the garage door opened and a fire red convertible pulled out. Rachel reclined in the passenger seat while her attractive, affectionate husband drove them off to what was clearly some wildly romantic dinner.

Melissa turned off the music and grabbed her backpack, suddenly reconsidering her all black outfit. She spotted her DoorDash hat and sweater in the backseat and pulled them on, along with a mask she still had in her glove box from COVID times. As she got out of the car and walked toward Rachel's house, her heart thudded loudly in her chest.

Then she saw the video doorbell.

"My bad, wrong address. I'm a DoorDash driver. Okay... bye," Melissa said, lowering her voice. She backed away and circled the house, spotting a door on the side of the garage. She twisted the knob, expecting it to be locked, but to her shock and delight, it swung open.

Standing inside the garage, Melissa realized she was officially breaking and entering. Swallowing the adrenaline, she pulled off her DoorDash sweater and hat, stuffing them into her bag and swapping them for her camera. She walked into the house, quickly checking for an alarm system. Another lucky break. None.

She began taking photos.

The walls were lined with shrines to Rachel Moore's life and accomplishments. Rachel and her husband on luxury vacations. Rachel receiving business awards. Awards for golfing, fishing, and achievements so excessive Melissa wondered if Rachel ever just sat on her couch and watched TV. How did she have the energy to never stop? These thoughts ran through her mind as she planted bugs in lamps in the living room and kitchen. Once she felt confident the downstairs was covered, she moved upstairs.

As she climbed the stairs, her hatred grew. Rachel had used her as a launchpad, a casualty in her rise to the top. And what a top it was. Luxury vacations, Kardashian level living. Melissa muttered, "This bitch," under her breath.

She walked into the primary bedroom. A massive California king canopy bed sat centered in the room, minimalist but somehow still obnoxiously extra. It took everything in Melissa not to vandalize it. She planted another bug in a lamp. She only had one left, so she scanned for the right spot and found Rachel's home office.

"What in the narcissism is this bullshit?"

Rachel Moore's office was perfectly curated. A gold and white desk sat in the center. Dual built-in shelves behind it were lined with awards, expensive looking vases, and books on finance, politics, and history. Between the shelves, prominently lit and expertly framed, hung a life sized portrait of Rachel.

Melissa rubbed her eyes. "It's fucking oil paint. Seriously?"

She snapped a photo as proof. Then, fueled by fresh rage, she installed her final bug in the desk lamp. She glanced at Rachel's computer and wished she'd thought about hacking, but her tech skills were firmly average Millennial. Which meant she was a wizard to Boomers and barely competent to Gen Z.

She turned to leave just as car headlights flashed across the window.

Panic flooded her body. She rushed to the glass and saw Rachel and her husband pulling into the garage. As the garage door echoed through the house, Melissa froze. Without thinking, she opened the office window and climbed onto the roof. She'd just shut the window and ducked aside when Rachel stormed into the room.

"Babe, there's no one here. Karen is just being a Karen. She thinks every delivery driver or lemonade stand is..." Rachel said, pulling up the door cam footage on her computer. "Yeah, it's just some DoorDash loser who can't use GPS."

She stood up, furious. "Date night ruined. I'm calling Karen and telling her to fuck right off."

Melissa exhaled in relief. Then the reality of her situation hit.

She was on a roof.

Option one, lower herself and drop. Option two, give up and confess. Option three, jump to the nearby tree and shimmy down. Option two was immediately off the table.

She almost chose option one but suddenly didn't trust her arms. Trusting her legs felt easier.

She jumped.

To her shock, she grabbed the branch. Then came the cracking sound. Then the snap. Melissa fell, the branch breaking part of her fall before she slammed into the ground. Fueled by adrenaline alone, she shoved the branch off and sprinted to her car, praying no cameras, neighbors, or Karen had seen her awkward escape.

Chapter 13: Clueless

Melissa's only real option was to go to Stone's Throw for first aid supplies. On the drive, she wondered if that guy would be there. He'd been kinder than the average store employee, but she worried he'd ask questions. It was bad enough imagining explaining this to Sloan or her mom. Somehow telling a younger, attractive man felt worse.

She walked into the store and sighed with relief when she saw an older woman at the register. Heading straight to the first aid aisle, she assessed her injuries. Cuts. Bruises. Nothing broken. Her ankle hurt, but she could still put weight on it.

Focused on supplies, Melissa didn't notice Logan spot her or hear him change course toward her.

"Want me to hook you up at the pharmacy?" Logan said as she reached for an ankle wrap.

Her startled reaction was reward enough for him.

"Wait, what? Can you do that?" Melissa asked, unsure whether to accept pills from a stranger, though it wouldn't be her biggest crime of the night.

Logan smiled and shook his head. "No, I can't. Figured a PI like you would know only a doctor can do that."

He gave her a once over and noticed she was genuinely hurt. "You need to RICE."

Seeing her confusion, he continued. "R, rest the injured limb. I, ice the area. C, compress it. That wrap should work. Then E, elevate your ankle above your heart. Plus, ibuprofen and Tylenol."

"Thanks," Melissa said, grabbing the items.

Logan didn't move. Instead, he added a reusable ice pack to her arms.

"I assume you have pillows at home?" he said, locking eyes with her.

Melissa stumbled over words until Logan couldn't take it anymore. "You know what, it's on the house."

"I'm very confused. Can't you get fired for this?" Melissa asked as she followed him toward the front of the store.

"I have an in with the owners. Don't worry about it," Logan said, trying to be casual and cool. He was pretty sure he was nailing it.

At the front, Melissa glanced at his name tag. "You're a very interesting person, Logan. Thank you."

She turned toward the automatic doors.

"I didn't catch your name," Logan said. "You don't have a name tag."

"Melissa."

He liked it. "Melissa the PI. Maybe I can help you with a case sometime. Sounds like an interesting line of work."

"I haven't told you anything..." Melissa began.

"I think it sounds interesting," Logan said, smiling.

She couldn't stop herself from returning a small smile. "Sure, maybe. But I should go... RICE now."

"Bet. Thanks for shopping local. Suck it, Wallyworld. You lost another one," Logan shouted as she left.

In hindsight, he realized he went too big with the exit line, but it still felt good, especially when he heard her laugh. He walked back through the aisles wondering who Melissa really was.

Meanwhile, Melissa was counting the seconds until she made it home. She didn't even consider what Cheryl might be doing.

Cheryl was currently in the arms of Daryl, a man she'd describe as a wonderful distraction. Fun for a Saturday night, but not someone she planned a future with. Even as she kissed him, she felt nothing more than lust, and even that was dampened by the overwhelming smell of his beard oil. It was aggressively fragrant, and she couldn't stop thinking about it. Combined with mediocre kissing, she was already leaning toward ending the night early.

Then Melissa burst through the front door.

While Cheryl knew her daughter would be horrified, she was relieved for the easy exit.

"Daryl, you need to leave. Honey, what happened?" Cheryl said, pushing him off and rushing toward Melissa, who was limping to the bathroom.

Daryl clutched his jacket. Melissa clocked the scene. "Date going well?"

"Eh. Fairly middle of the road. Too much beard oil. It felt like I was kissing a cinnamon stick," Cheryl said while inspecting her daughter.

Daryl started gathering his things, then paused. "Should I call you?"

Cheryl didn't respond.

"Should I call you later?" he asked louder.

"Do what feels right. Bye," Cheryl said without looking up.

After the door closed, Cheryl helped Melissa to her bed. "Take off your clothes. I need to see if you need the ER."

"Oh my god, you do not need to take me to the ER," Melissa said, rolling her eyes but changing into an oversized sleep shirt.

Cheryl returned with rubbing alcohol and cotton balls. "Do you feel nauseous or really thirsty?" She pressed Melissa's stomach. "Does this hurt?"

"Only the bruises. Mom, I'm not dying," Melissa said. "I fell while exercising, landed on some shrubbery, and twisted my ankle. It's not a big deal."

"You look like you were in a car accident," Cheryl said, checking her forehead and hands. "You're not clammy. Good. I'm getting ice and pillows."

Melissa endured the wound cleaning with only a few tears. Cheryl didn't ask more questions, just kept tisking at the injuries like they'd personally offended her. By the time she reached the last cut, the Tylenol and ice had kicked in and exhaustion rolled over Melissa.

"Do you want a blanket or a snack?" Cheryl asked.

Melissa nodded, but by the time Cheryl returned with a blanket and cookie, she was asleep. Cheryl draped the blanket over her and ate the cookie while watching her daughter. She was deeply concerned. She'd even reached out to Dr. David.

He'd told her she couldn't force treatment unless Melissa was a danger to herself or others, but that he'd see her again if Melissa wanted. That had comforted Cheryl, but she still wondered if she'd recognize danger if it came.

She went to her room, pulled out her phone, and texted Sloan asking her to come check on Melissa. Sloan immediately agreed, giving Cheryl hope that maybe this was rock bottom. And if it was, there was nowhere to go but up.

That was enough for Cheryl to finally fall asleep, just in time to miss a text from Daryl saying he couldn't stop thinking about her. In the morning, she'd laugh. It was always the men she showed the least interest in who fell the hardest.

Chapter 14: Booksmart

Melissa woke to sunlight streaming across her face. She considered rolling over until pain reminded her her ankle was injured and her whole body hurt. As she assessed whether getting up was worth it, she heard her mom's voice talking about coffee, followed by Sloan's.

"That coffee smells amazing... I miss caffeine."

"I drank coffee throughout my pregnancy and Melissa was fine. Want a cup? I promise not to tell Zach," Cheryl said.

Sloan was about to cave when Melissa fell to the floor, sending both women rushing to her room. Melissa had pulled herself to her knees by the time they arrived.

"Morning, sunshine," Sloan said as Melissa hauled herself back onto the bed.

"No one knocks. I could have been vagina out," Melissa said.

"Well, then I would have seen your vagina," Sloan said, unfazed.

Melissa began to protest, but Sloan continued. "I don't want to see yours either, but sometimes you see other people's vaginas. That's life."

"I've seen most of my friends' vaginas," Cheryl added.

Sloan gestured to Cheryl, and Melissa made a noise of disgust.

"Coffee? Or more ice for that ankle?" Cheryl offered.

"Ice," Melissa said.

"You promise not to tell Zach?" Sloan asked.

"My alliance is with you. Screw Zach and his caffeine denial nonsense," Cheryl said, leaving to get coffee and ice.

Once Cheryl was out of earshot, Sloan turned to Melissa. "So I know that you know that I know you didn't get these injuries from exercise. Your mom didn't buy it either, just FYI."

"You told me to work through my shit. This was an accident from doing that," Melissa said, reaching for more Tylenol.

"Mel, what does that mean?" Sloan asked.

Before Melissa could answer, Cheryl bustled back in with coffee, ice, and toast, which she forced Melissa to eat. Cheryl fussed over her ankle while Sloan waited, anxiety simmering. The conversation drifted to pregnancy, and Sloan accidentally mentioned making Melissa the baby's godmother.

"I'm going to be a god grandmother?" Cheryl gasped.

"I hadn't thought about it like that, but I guess," Sloan said. "More love can't hurt."

Melissa stayed quiet, feeling oddly disconnected.

"I'm making a baby blanket. Do you know the sex? Never mind, neutral. Just not yellow. Too bright," Cheryl rambled, then caught herself. "I'm going on too much, aren't I?"

"I'm sure it'll be perfect," Sloan said sincerely.

"You're a doll. I'll leave you girls to talk," Cheryl said, closing the door behind her.

Sloan sat beside Melissa. "How did this really happen?"

Melissa told the truth, downplaying the danger but failing to make jumping off a roof and falling out of a tree sound reasonable.

"You jumped off a roof?" Sloan said flatly.

"Well, it was that or stay up there overnight and get caught," Melissa said.

"I think the real option was not committing a B and E at your middle school bully's house," Sloan shot back. When Melissa tried to argue, Sloan stopped her. "I know I said you don't know what's going on in people's lives, but why do you need to know about hers? We're not kids. You could get into serious trouble."

"Rachel Moore didn't mildly bully me. I became Moppy. I was a puddle for three years until she got expelled after a teacher saw her pouring water into my backpack and I slipped down a staircase. I could have died," Melissa said.

"She got expelled. That was the karma. It already happened," Sloan said.

"She has a perfect life. How is expulsion enough after trying to kill me?" Melissa snapped.

"How perfect?" Sloan asked, running out of arguments.

Melissa grabbed her backpack, pulled out her camera, and handed it over. "Look at these. She has a life sized oil painting of herself."

Sloan clicked through the photos, then sighed. "I'm going to help you. But, and this is a big but, you cannot act like a deranged muppet. No more roofs."

"Deal."

"I need to go home. This coffee is destroying me. But come over later. Zach has a work thing. We can plot," Sloan said.

Knowing Sloan couldn't poop at other people's houses, Melissa let her go. Alone again, she pulled out her laptop and checked the bugs.

They worked.

Chapter 15: Knives Out

Melissa felt childlike excitement. Being able to overhear her arch nemesis felt like Christmas morning. Except she was the one in the big red suit who came down the chimney by breaking in through the garage door.

The software only saved recordings when sound was detected and time coded them, which helped, but she still sifted through plenty of nothing. To stay entertained, Melissa imagined Rachel doing ridiculous things.

"Babe, are there any oranges left? Babe? Oranges? Are there any oranges left? I'll get them my damn self," Rachel yelled. In Melissa's mind, she lounged on a chaise in a toga.

Melissa clicked the next file.

"Cry me a river, yeah yeah, you don't have to say what you did, I already know, I heard it from..." Rachel sang off key. Melissa imagined a skincare routine filmed like a Neutrogena ad and skipped it immediately.

"Yes, obviously we need to raise rates if margins are that close. Thank you for interrupting my time with a question a four year old would know the answer to," Rachel snapped. Melissa pictured her doing eighties aerobics in neon spandex.

More clips rolled by. Some made Melissa laugh. Most made her hate Rachel more. After hours, she started losing hope.

Then she heard it.

"Hello, you," Rachel purred.

Goosebumps rose on Melissa's arms. This was it.

"No, my husband is in the next room, so we have to be sexy quiet. Ohhh, then what are you going to do? Yeah, then I'll bring the Cool Whip. Yes, Cool Whip, it tastes better. Don't ruin this. I'll see you on the twenty sixth at the Ritz Carlton at seven sharp, you big sexy man you."

"There you are, you demon weasel," Melissa shouted, fist pumping. "I knew you were a vapid soulless monster."

She grabbed her laptop and limped for the car. Cheryl shouted after her to stay off her ankle, but pain was secondary to vengeance.

Melissa pounded so hard on Sloan's front door that Zach opened it in a panic, shirt half buttoned, eyes wild. Melissa shoved past him.

"Well hello to you too," Zach snapped. "You almost gave me a heart attack."

"Where's Sloan?" Melissa asked, then frowned. "Why are you here? I thought you had a work thing?"

"She's peeing. I'm on my way out," Zach said, grabbing his keys. He hesitated, considering whether to say something, but then Sloan appeared. "There she is. Bye, honey."

He kissed Sloan and left.

Melissa told Sloan everything and played the recording. Sloan tried to match her excitement but couldn't hide her concern.

"You planted bugs? You broke into her house?" Sloan said.

"Okay, so I'm like a shitty Batman," Melissa said. "She's meeting a guy at the Ritz Carlton."

"So you got your answer. She's still awful. Now you can stop," Sloan said, stress eating crackers.

"No. Karma clearly needs help. I'm balancing her scales," Melissa said.

"No breaking and entering," Sloan said.

"Light breaking and entering. Hotels don't count," Melissa offered.

"To catch a cheater and stop your spiral, I'll help plan. But I'm not helping you break the law," Sloan said. "So how are you getting proof?"

They argued strategies for nearly an hour.

"Under no circumstances can you enter anyone's room. Common areas are gray. Rooms are a hard no," Sloan said.

"Fine," Melissa said, staring at the counter, unsure if she meant it.

"What if we do your baby shower there?" Melissa suddenly said. "Jenna's husband is rich. Tell Brooke you want a spa night and she'll get Jenna to..."

"I just wanted a classic baby shower where people buy me stuff so I don't panic about money," Sloan said sheepishly. "Plus Brooke already planned it for this Friday. Your invite went out."

"Wow. Short notice," Melissa said, hurt flaring. "You didn't want me to help?"

"You had a lot going on. I told Brooke a while ago. I didn't announce it," Sloan said, rubbing her stomach. "I'm also not getting smaller."

Melissa forced a laugh.

"We don't have to get into that. What if I pay for the room?" Sloan offered.

"No. I'll pay. It's my project. What are credit cards for?" Melissa blurted. "Maybe Mr. Rachel Moore will pay me for the photos."

Sloan watched her closely. Melissa felt exposed. Being around Sloan while knowing she wasn't okay made her anxiety spike. Before Sloan could say anything, Melissa stood up.

"Oh wow, I lost track of time. I should go. Sorry."

"Mel, I love you," Sloan said.

"Yeah, love you too," Melissa mumbled, not turning around as she waved and left.

In her car, Melissa finally felt alone. Her mom and Sloan cared, but it made it harder to feel her feelings. Maybe she really was losing it. Maybe she should drop this whole thing.

She turned on the engine and radio, letting the noise quiet her mind. All she had to do was get home. Then she could decide.

Then Rachel Moore's Mercedes drove past blasting Ava Max's Sweet but Psycho.

Melissa stared.

If that wasn't a sign from the universe, what was?

She pulled out of her parking spot and followed Rachel.

For a moment, Melissa wondered if she'd crossed a line. Was this where she became the villain instead of the hero? She wasn't going to kidnap or kill her. She briefly imagined kidnapping Rachel and doing some light psychological warfare, but quickly abandoned that fantasy when she realized it only ended in death or prison.

So what was the plan? Why was she following her?

Rachel pulled into the parking lot of RM Consulting and Management. She didn't use her turn signal, which irritated Melissa. She parked far enough away not to be noticed but wondered how often apex predators worried about being watched.

Melissa turned off the engine and stared at the sleek, modern building. New money screamed from its dark glass and steel frame. There was no obvious sign, just a gold placard by the door that read RM Consulting and Management.

She pulled the heavy door open and stepped inside.

Chapter 16: The Devil Wears Prada

The inside was just as ostentatious and sleek as the outside. Minimalistic and modern, every piece of furniture and decoration meticulously chosen to make sure anyone walking inside the building would feel insignificant. A receptionist stood behind a desk with a headset on in the middle of a call. He was young, dressed in a suit Melissa was sure was designer, with a perfectly manicured beard that looked like it had been modeled after Cena Crane from The Hunger Games.

"Yes, Miss Moore has that on her schedule, but she is currently off site with another client. Of course, Miss Moore will call you back as soon as she is able. Thank you for calling RM Consulting and Management. Have a wonderful day."

He clicked the phone off as soon as his speech concluded, then spotted Melissa, contempt entering his face. Melissa became acutely aware of everything she was wearing, how her hair was undone, and that makeup had not crossed her mind since the breakup, which was probably making this man deeply uncomfortable. So obviously, it was now his job to make her just as uncomfortable.

"Welcome to RM Consulting. How can I assist you today?" His words without tone could have passed as polite, but his delivery made Melissa very aware that he thought she was lost and wished she would leave.

Melissa wondered if she should, but she had decided before opening the door that maybe she was supposed to talk to

Rachel Moore again. Alone. No pressure. Give her the opportunity to make amends. If she had to endure this unpleasant interaction, she could do it.

"Oh, funny story. I actually know Rachel. We were schoolmates. I thought since I was in the neighborhood, I would say hello," Melissa said, attempting to sound calm and collected.

The receptionist looked her up and down, confusion now entering his contempt. "Really? You went to Columbia?"

"Oh no, we went to middle school together," Melissa conceded.

The receptionist smirked. "Name?"

"Melissa. But she would remember me as Moppy. It was a fun school nickname."

The instant stomachache that came with saying the nickname prevented Melissa from noticing the smugness spreading across the receptionist's face. He pressed a few buttons on his headset and waited for only two rings.

"Hello, Miss Moore. A Moppy is here to see you."

There were a few beats while he listened to Rachel's reply. Surprise crossed his face. "Really. All right, I'll show her to your office."

Melissa followed him down a long hallway, every footstep echoing. She wondered if Rachel had built this place with psychological games already in mind, or if she had simply chosen it because of them. The receptionist opened the door and gestured for Melissa to walk through without a word.

Rachel was standing, leaning against her desk, arms crossed. Behind her hung multiple business articles with photos of Rachel in the same pose. For a moment, Melissa lost herself staring at them. Then she almost laughed. Was this really her move, and more importantly, did it really work on clients?

"Moppy, what a pleasant, though unexpected surprise!" Rachel's voice rang out, snapping Melissa back to the present. "Impeccable timing. I just got in. Two run ins in a week. Are you stalking me?"

The question sent a shiver down Melissa's spine, but Rachel laughed at her own joke, so Melissa joined her. When the moment calmed, she answered, "No. No stalking. I just needed to ask you a few things that came to mind after we bumped into each other."

"Well, time is money, and my time is more valuable than most. What's on your mind?" Rachel asked. Melissa felt scanned, like Rachel was searching for weak points. At the moment, Melissa couldn't help but feel like Rachel had too much to work with.

"It'll be quick. Did you really not remember me?" Melissa said, unable to find a better place to start.

Rachel nodded knowingly, like she had expected the question. "Oh, so this is that chat. Look, Moppy"

"Melissa," Melissa interrupted.

Rachel smiled, but it didn't feel kind. It felt like Melissa had somehow fallen into her trap. She instantly regretted standing up for herself. Seeking justice was easier when she wasn't under Rachel's crippling gaze.

"Really. Okay, Melissa. We were kids. I think the teachers overreacted with the whole expulsion thing, but honestly, it really worked out for me. So if you want to apologize"

"Apologize. Me?" Melissa said, her mind reeling at the implication. She had been hospitalized because of what Rachel did to her. How was Rachel so easily twisting the truth?

"For snitching on me, yeah. But look, it's not necessary. It put me on the path to where I am today. Which, if you don't mind a little bragging on my end, is pretty fucking great," Rachel said, ending with a sly wink.

Melissa looked around the office, at the accolades and achievements that made Rachel Moore seem untouchable. Rachel was baiting her, craving a reaction.

"My parents forced me into golf to keep me busy, which got me a full ride. I nearly went pro. But I wanted a career with boundlessness, so I started this company. My company. I married a puppy dog of a trophy husband who took my last name. I mean, who could change a name like Rachel Moore? Besides, his last name was Clampitt. It was his only flaw. He's happier as a Moore."

"That's amazing," Melissa said, barely trying to hide her defeat.

Rachel took her seat behind the desk and assessed her. "What about you? Married? You look like you have kids."

Part of Melissa wondered if Rachel just wanted more ammunition, but another part couldn't find a reason not to answer. What could Rachel say that she hadn't already thought? Still, a sick feeling brewed in her stomach. This was why Rachel didn't deserve her life. She was emotionally slapping Melissa for sport, kicking a dead horse, and yet Melissa told the truth anyway.

"No. I lost my job. Basically, the company I worked for, Evergreen Solutions, didn't pay back an EIDL loan, and it turned out the owner had done some illegal things to try to keep the business afloat. So it's been hard to find work when the only real job you had as an adult is tied to that."

"Jesus, you were at Evergreen? Christ, those fuckers tried to hire me about a year ago, but I told them the best thing they could do was shut down and that I wouldn't let my name be associated with them," Rachel said, her swagger uninterrupted. Unbeknownst to Melissa, Rachel felt a flicker of sympathy, though she would never show it. Curiosity won out anyway. "Did you ever find a guy or girl? It looks like you have kids."

Was she covered in jelly? Did her purse look like a diaper bag? Had her weight fluctuated enough to make someone think she was pregnant? All of this ran through Melissa's mind as she tried to answer.

"Nope. My college boyfriend Jeremy, after eight years, decided to cheat on me. He's going to be a father to their child. I keep seeing Facebook updates about how doting he is.”

“Moppy, it really sounds like you need a little sweet revenge,” Rachel said. Somehow, it was the kindest thing she had said all day, which confused Melissa because it was exactly what she had been planning. “I’m going to give you some advice. Some shrinks might disagree. You need to get some agency back. Stand up for yourself. Grab life by the pussy and fuck some shit up.”

“Yeah?” Melissa said, a genuine smile crossing her face. Suddenly, Rachel felt more like a life coach. Maybe this was karma delivering a message straight from the bully’s mouth. The universe giving her permission. She needed to fuck some shit up, specifically Rachel’s shit.

“Fuck yeah,” Rachel said, then scribbled something on a sticky note. Melissa barely noticed, lost in thought, until the scratching of pen on paper pulled her back.

“I think I needed this chat. You showed me who you are, and I think it helped me realize I should trust my gut,” Melissa said, smiling.

“Well, I’d also lose some of that gut too. A revenge body would be impressive,” Rachel said, standing. The gesture was clear. Time was up.

“I should let you get back to work. It was good catching up with you,” Melissa said, surprised to mean it.

Rachel walked her to the door and handed her a bone white, gold embossed business card. “My standard rate is two hundred an hour plus a fifteen hundred retainer, but for Moppy, I'm sure we could work something out."

Melissa let it roll off her. This was proof Rachel deserved karma. She had not grown. She had been rewarded for cruelty. Melissa was going to be the force that knocked her off the pedestal she had built for herself.

"Thank you for the clarity," Melissa said, turning toward the reception area.

Behind her, Rachel was already on the phone again.

The receptionist now looked at Melissa with mild curiosity instead of contempt but said nothing as she passed.

Walking to her car, Melissa couldn't shake the feeling that Rachel was watching her. She replayed the conversation in her mind, the insults threading their way into her subconscious, waiting to surface when she was weakest. Driving away, she knew she needed a plan. She felt too energized to go home and face her mother, and Sloan would ask too many questions she didn't have answers to.

So Melissa drove.

She put distance between herself and Rachel until the air felt breathable again. Eventually, she pulled into the parking lot of a place that looked like a slowly decaying tiki bar and decided to go in alone. Normally, the thought would make her skin crawl. Today, it felt right.

Chapter 17: Fool's Gold

The name of the slowly decaying tiki bar was Fool's Gold. The decor looked like someone had mashed pirates, buried treasure, and Polynesian tribal patterns together. It was a lot, but it also looked like the kind of place that could make a fun fruity drink, so it would do.

Since it was only four in the afternoon, only a handful of people were inside. Melissa didn't feel bad about taking an entire booth far from the karaoke stage, where one sad girl was poorly singing an Adele song at her passed out boyfriend, and far from the bar, where an older man muttered into his beer.

Melissa dug into her purse for her wallet and a pen. As if the scent of cash summoned her, a harassed looking woman in her late twenties wearing a Hawaiian-style dress and a name tag reading Aloha appeared.

"Is your name really Aloha?" Melissa asked.

"No, but it helps keep creeps from learning more about me than they need to," she said bluntly.

Melissa respected the hell out of that. "What can I get you?"

"Hale Pele Mai Tai. And do you have a pad of paper I could use?" Melissa said quickly, grabbing the menu.

Aloha sighed but nodded and walked away.

As Melissa waited, anxiety crept back in. The conversation with Rachel that had pumped her up already felt distant.

The karaoke girl switched to an Alanis Morissette song, clearly working through something, which somehow messed with Melissa's confidence even more.

Then Aloha set the Hale Pele in front of her, and Melissa did something she had not done since her early twenties. She lifted the drink and drained it before Aloha had even dropped the notebook on the table.

"Can I have another?"

"Please don't puke in the bar area," Aloha said pleadingly.

Melissa nodded solemnly. "I promise."

"I'll get you another one."

Melissa settled in and started trying to come up with a foolproof revenge plan, weaving in Sloan's advice. No matter how many Hale Peles she drank, she knew one thing for sure. She would not survive prison. She did not have the physical or mental skills for a smooth correctional facility experience. Plus, orange would never be her new black. It made her look pale, malnourished, and somehow heavier than she was. If Rachel was to be believed, Melissa needed to avoid that at all costs.

The problem was she couldn't figure out how to get into Rachel's hotel room without some version of breaking and entering, and she definitely could not afford a night at the Ritz. Rachel's income might sustain her lifestyle, but Melissa wasn't about to go into debt over revenge.

She considered applying for a job at the hotel. Housekeepers had access to every room. Then reality hit. There wasn't time to apply, get hired, and gain access.

She wrote plans, tore them up, and added them to a growing pile of failures. Six Hale Peles later, she was stumped.

The frosted window she could see from her booth turned out to be the front door, and by the darkness outside, she could tell it was night. The bar hadn't filled much more, but the karaoke girl and her boyfriend were gone.

Aloha swung by her table. "Another, or do you want me to call someone for you?"

She eyed the crumpled papers. "You're not writing a suicide note, right?"

Melissa stared at her. "I'm trying to get revenge without breaking the law. I'm not suicidal."

"I'm switching you to water," Aloha said.

Melissa raised one pleading finger.

Aloha sighed. "Fine. One more. Then water only. And you're ordering a sandwich."

"You're the best," Melissa said sincerely.

Just then, the front door swung open and a bachelor party stumbled in. Hawaiian shirts everywhere.

Melissa froze.

Among them was Logan.

She stared, briefly distracted by how unfairly good he looked in a neon pink floral shirt and board shorts. Then he spotted her. She dove behind the menu.

Logan laughed. He told one of his friends he would be back and headed over, casually running a hand through his hair in a way that was meant to look effortless and absolutely did not.

"Hey there, PI lady," Logan said, sliding into the booth across from her.

"No, a PI," Melissa corrected, mortified.

"No, you're not a bounty hunter. Remember? It's our whole bit," Logan said cheerfully.

"You're a very nice kid"

"Ouch. I'll have you know I'm a whole ass adult. Job, 401k, apartment, whole nine," Logan said.

"So says your fake ID," Melissa shot back just as Aloha arrived with her drink, water, and sandwich. "You should check his ID."

"Did I hear fake ID?" Aloha said, narrowing her eyes at Logan.

He smoothly pulled out his wallet. "Ma'am, it's as real as the birthmark on my butt."

Melissa nearly died.

Aloha took the ID. Logan turned to Melissa with a wink, which unfortunately reminded her of Rachel Moore.

"Logan Cooper Stone, born June sixth, nineteen ninety seven, Gemini, I live at fifteen ninety eight East Emery Street"

"Yeah, yeah. Whatever, Romeo. What can I get you?" Aloha said, handing the ID back.

"Whatever beer you have on tap. Put it on that guy in the yellow Hawaiian shirt with the birds," Logan said.

"You're like seven years younger than me," Melissa muttered.

"Cougar. Sweet," Logan said.

"I'm not a cougar. I'm not chasing you," Melissa said, shoving a bite of fried chicken sandwich into her mouth.

"What a shame," Logan sighed theatrically.

"Logan, if you're going to go for an older woman, maybe go for one who hasn't been lying to you," Melissa said through a second bite.

"Lying? So you're telling me you're not a PI?" Logan said with enough sarcasm that even drunk Melissa caught it. Then he softened. "I mean, you didn't know where to buy PI gear or basic pharmacy laws, so I assumed it wasn't your real job."

"I can't even pull off lying to a grocery store employee," Melissa said, annoyed with herself as she downed her last Aloha approved drink.

"I'm working at my parents' store because my dad shattered his hip falling off a ladder. Lucky for me, a mildly insane, very pretty lady walked in my first week, and now we're here," Logan said, smiling too brightly on purpose.

Any other day, it might have melted her. Today, her stomach made all decisions.

"I'm going to be sick," Melissa said, bolting for the bathroom.

The bachelor party howled with laughter.

"Wow, she saw your face and that's what made her puke?" someone shouted.

"That's not how your mom feels!" Logan yelled back, following her.

Melissa barely made it. She dropped to her knees in front of the toilet, every ounce of her dignity dissolving. Things she thought were long digested made surprise reappearances.

The bathroom door opened.

"Pardon any women in the bathroom. I'm just checking on Melissa," Logan said.

"Oh, for fuck's sake, I'm the only one in here," Melissa sputtered.

Logan grabbed paper towels, ran cold water over them, and handed them to her, then took a few steps back to give her space.

"Thanks," Melissa muttered, wiping her face. The cold towel felt better than it had any right to.

"I'm trying to ruin my middle school bully's life," she blurted.

"Strange choice. I don't think puking will help much," Logan said carefully.

"No, she's cheating on her husband. Everyone thinks her life is perfect, but she's awful. She thought I should apologize to her because she" Melissa paused, nausea and alcohol colliding. "I did everything right. I was good. And I'm here on the floor of a bar, puking in front of a cute guy, not married, not pregnant, no career. If I'm good, why do I suffer? If she's bad, why does she get everything? She hurts people for sport. She even hurts her puppy dog husband by cheating."

"I mean, still not great, but she's not serial killer bad. Why not tell her husband?" Logan asked gently.

"He'll need proof. Something she can't wiggle out of. She's slippery," Melissa said.

"And being drunk on a bathroom floor helps how?" Logan asked, kneeling closer.

"It doesn't. I just can't figure out how to get into the hotel without spending hundreds I don't have. I'm a DoorDasher.

A college educated DoorDasher who sleeps in her childhood bedroom because her life fell apart. And the first guy to even kind of look at me like I'm worth something is watching me monologue with vomit breath and sweaty hair."

She smiled darkly, waiting for him to retreat.

Instead, Logan helped her to her feet and only let go when she was steady. "I'm taking you home. Not in a sexy way. In a human way. You need to be home."

"I need a plan," Melissa said weakly.

"Sleep. Aspirin. Food. Then plans," Logan said calmly.

She nodded.

Then passed out.

"Oh boy," Logan muttered.

Aloha walked in and assessed the scene, then looked at Logan. "You look like a Dateline special."

"I know," Logan said. "Yellow shirt's tab. And you should absolutely add a forty percent gratuity and tell them it's a bachelor party policy."

Aloha nodded. She had student loans.

Chapter 18: The Gentleman

Melissa woke in confusion on unfamiliar sheets draped over a couch. Beside her sat an empty plastic bin, an unopened bottle of water, and aspirin. Her face felt heavy. From the kitchen came soft rock music, the smell of bacon, and warm sunlight spilling through the room.

"Where am I?" she croaked.

Logan stepped out of the kitchen, whisking eggs in board shorts and no Hawaiian shirt. "My couch. Technically my apartment. Hope you like scrambled eggs."

Melissa looked around and spotted her shirt in the corner. She was wearing a baggy World of Warcraft shirt instead. Panic flickered.

"We didn't"

"Oh yeah, we totally passionately slept in separate rooms," Logan said lightly. "I figured you wouldn't want to sleep covered in vomit, so I did that trick girls do when they take off a bra without removing their shirt, but with two shirts."

"I slept on the couch?"

"Yeah. That was selfish, but it would have been easier to clean if you puked more," Logan said, pouring eggs into a pan.

Melissa checked herself. Everything except the shirt was still on. Logan was officially not a creep. She briefly wondered how low the bar for men was, then abandoned the thought.

"You live here?" she asked.

"Bought it about a year ago."

"You can afford this working at your parents' store?" Melissa asked, realizing too late it sounded rude.

"I said I was helping out while my dad recovers. I didn't say that's my job, ya gold digger," Logan said, teasing.

"Thanks for everything, but I should probably"

"Run away?" Logan asked, setting plates on a tiny table. "We agreed last night in the toilets that you'd eat and take aspirin first. I'm holding up my end. These are elite scrambled eggs. I also have hot sauce. I use ketchup."

"So do I. Wait." Melissa frowned. "You could be plotting my murder. I don't even know where I am."

"Fifteen ninety-eight East Emery Street. Five minute walk from the bar. Ten if you're carrying a body," Logan said.

"I don't remember much from last night," Melissa admitted, sitting.

"Well, I promised to help you plan revenge against your middle school bully if you slept and ate. So you're halfway there," he said sincerely.

"You mean it?" Melissa asked. "You want to help?"

"I'd like to hang out with you sober and without me wearing a smock," Logan said, squeezing ketchup onto his eggs. "Is that terrible?"

"You're weird," Melissa said.

"You're weirder, but I like it."

They ate. Almost like normal people.

Her stomach limited her enthusiasm, but it tasted good. The quiet gave her time to think about Jeremy again. He had never cooked her breakfast, unless pop tarts counted, and even then only because he wanted one and not the other. Logan felt different. Light. Kind. Jeremy's jokes had always sharpened instead of softened.

She realized how many tiny things she had stopped doing for Jeremy. Eating eggs with ketchup. Reading physical books. Leaving clothing tags on. Little things that chipped away at her confidence. She had known Logan for less than a day, but she already felt he would never do that.

"This was really good," Melissa said.

"Thanks," Logan said, grinning as he carried plates to the sink. "Tell me about the bully. Catch me up."

"Okay. It started when my friend Sloan announced she was pregnant, which was shocking because we hadn't talked much lately. I was getting over a breakup. Sorry, I won't talk about him"

"I don't care if it's part of the story," Logan said, pouring coffee. "Want some?"

"Please. Okay, his name is Jeremy. He cheated. It's over. Anyway, at Sloan's brunch, I ran into my middle school bully, Rachel Moore."

"That name sounds like a bully. She's blonde, right?" Logan said.

"She is. So I did a background check and found out she's thriving. Like American Dream thriving. Then, after your suggestions"

"You're welcome," Logan said, raising his mug.

"I found out she's having an affair. So I want proof for her husband. She calls him her trophy husband who took her last name. Which is fine, but the way she says it feels like a power move."

"Do you know the guy she's cheating with?" Logan asked.

"No. I just know they're meeting at the Ritz on the twenty sixth. A Saturday. I have Sloan's baby shower Friday."

Logan noticed her zoning out and gently touched her hand. She blinked back.

"It just feels like a lot," Logan said. "She hasn't been in your life for years. You're not trying to hurt her physically or anything"

"No," Melissa said firmly. "I'm not making anything up either. Just proof and telling her husband. I know it sounds crazy, but I need to settle the karmic score."

Logan thought it over. If she was telling the truth, she just wanted to tell a guy his wife was cheating. There was a good chance he already suspected. And while she had lied to him, she had been comically bad at it, and she had not owed him anything. Plus, that Jeremy guy clearly did damage.

"Okay," Logan said slowly. "Long shot, but remember the guy in the yellow Hawaiian shirt?"

He handed her a wedding invitation from his fridge. "He's getting married on the twenty sixth. At the Ritz."

"You're shitting me," Melissa said, reading it.

"Nope. No shitting currently," Logan said. "I have a plus one. If you're willing to play cougar, we can sneak away and get your proof."

"A reason to be at the hotel that won't max out my credit card," Melissa said, relief washing over her.

Overwhelmed, she kissed him, invitation still in her hand. They pulled back, both surprised.

"Well damn. Zero chemistry," Logan said, not believing himself.

"Isn't that always the way?" Melissa said, smiling.

He kissed her again, and it was better.

She wanted to stay lost there, but her phone buzzed in her pocket. Reality returned. She had over a dozen missed calls from her mom and Sloan, plus texts from Brooke, Jenna, and Zach.

"I should go. I think I have an Amber Alert out on me," Melissa said, kissing Logan's cheek.

He helped her up.

She gathered her things and looked down at the shirt. "Any chance I could borrow something less nerdy?"

"Nerdy?" Logan asked.

"Just something that won't start questions."

He disappeared and returned with a plain white shirt. "Here."

"Thank you."

She changed, kissed him once more, and bolted out the door.

Both were disappointed by the derailment, but Melissa had found something she had not believed was possible anymore.

Hope.

Chapter 19: Inside Out

Melissa quickly texted everyone except her mother and Sloan. She had decided her mom would need an in-person confirmation of life and Sloan would need, at minimum, a phone call. By the time she made it to her car, Sloan was already playing through Bluetooth.

"Seriously, you disappeared? What the hell, Mel?" Sloan said, her voice strained with an attempt at calm.

Melissa stayed quiet. She wasn't sure what she wanted to share. Maybe Sloan would be happy to hear she'd met someone like Logan. Or maybe she'd judge her about the age gap and how they'd met, with him being a grocery store clerk. What if telling her ruined the one nice new thing she'd had since everything happened with Jeremy and Evergreen?

"Mel, can you please tell me where you are? I can come get you. We can"

"I'm not dead in a ditch, I just needed a break, some time to think," Melissa said as she started driving. As the sun beat down on her face, she fumbled for her sunglasses.

Sloan began laying into her more, but the words barely reached Melissa as she managed to find her sunglasses and shove them on. "You know, I get that you were worried. I'm really sorry about that. I didn't mean to scare anyone. I'm safe. I'm heading home. I'm sure my mom will read me the same riot act. So why don't you relax and stop stressing you and the baby out over me."

"That really sucked." Sloan's voice somehow managed to nail mom guilt, a skill Melissa didn't think she'd acquire until after the baby came. "If something happened to you, it'd kill me if, I love you, you know. And I know things haven't been easy for you recently, but you can't pull this kind of thing again."

"Heard. I won't. I'm sorry," Melissa said, not sure if it was a promise she'd keep but hoping she would. A tiny bit of shame seeped into the happiness she thought she'd found. "Hey, I'm really close to home and my phone is almost dead. I'm gonna go."

"Fine. Just text me later," Sloan said before hanging up. Bluetooth switched back to music.

The thumping beat of Rihanna's SOS was not the right song for Melissa's mood, so she turned it off, preferring quiet. Due to the nonstop overthinking Melissa was prone to, preferring quiet was rare enough that even she clocked the strangeness of wanting silence. Was it the hangover from all the Hale Peles, or was she feeling retrospective? Maybe both.

She felt like she had emotional whiplash. The high of Logan's attention and the discovery of an actual next step for her revenge plan had distracted her from her now familiar gloom and doom. That gloom and doom was constantly threatening to push its way to the front of her mind, always hovering in the background, inching closer. Thankfully, she had just pulled up to the house, so she fled the car and her feelings and went to face Cheryl instead.

Cheryl was elbow deep in knitting an aquamarine baby blanket. She was trying to keep things light, but Melissa could tell Sloan must have texted her because the cheerfulness felt almost too convincing.

"Oh sweetheart, you're home. Did you have a nice night out?" Cheryl said between knitting maneuvers. "Can you believe I'm actually going to finish this thing before the shower?"

Melissa walked over and touched a corner. It was soft and warm. She imagined her mom had yearned to make one for her for so long that it must have been a relief to make one for Sloan instead, like an emotional surrogate. A few flashes of jealousy bubbled up, but Melissa popped them before they could grow. Sloan had been through enough and deserved a homemade blanket and the baby that would follow.

Cheryl couldn't wait for Melissa to respond any longer. "Did I go too big?" She lifted the blanket. It was large enough to cover a twin sized bed, but the sudden wobble in confidence made Melissa softly smirk. "I went too big. I got over excited for Sloan."

"I'm sure she's going to love it," Melissa said. She leaned down, kissed her mom's head, then turned toward the kitchen. "I just wanted to say sorry about not answering my phone last night. I totally lost track of time and then my phone went on do not disturb, so I didn't even hear it ring"

Melissa's eyes landed on the refrigerator. A newly placed invitation was stuck on with a magnet. Sloan's baby shower.

It struck Melissa like a slap in the face, not because she hadn't been warned but because it was perfect. Simple ivory cardstock with a wreath of soft flowers framing delicate, easy to read writing. The card felt like proof that Sloan's life had improved without her. Melissa wouldn't have been able to pull this off.

"Please join us for Sloan's first baby, baby shower. Please RSVP with the mom to be's sister, Brooke" Melissa's mind read it in Brooke's warm, sassy voice. "And not that broke, dumb, and ugly friend of Sloan's Melissa. Bitch couldn't plan anything to save her life. None of us know why Sloan bothers with that loser. She only just told her she was even pregnant."

Melissa quickly wiped away the tear that had escaped as Cheryl noticed she'd seen the invite. She prayed Cheryl missed both the tear and the mood shift. The gloom and doom had found her again.

"It's wonderful, right?" Cheryl said cheerfully. When Melissa didn't respond right away, Cheryl noticed. "Honey?"

"Yeah, it's great. Brooke did a nice job," Melissa said, though even she could hear the wobble. Her carefully crafted act of being fine had slipped.

"And we can say the blanket is from us if you're worried about buying a gift for the shower," Cheryl said, swinging at what she thought might be the problem.

Melissa's internal spiral about being worthless wasn't soothed by this. If anything, it made her feel more like a burden. Her own mother didn't think she was capable of pulling off a simple shower gift. So how could Sloan have trusted her to be involved in planning the party? The only answers Melissa could find were couldn't, didn't, and would probably take her mom up on the blanket deal.

"You seemed happy a moment ago, but your face changed. Sweetheart, tell me what happened."

"I'm just really tired. I think I'm going to go take a nap." Melissa turned away from her mom and the fridge and retreated to the one place that felt safe, her bed.

The short walk from the kitchen to her room felt like miles. Closing the door behind her felt like pushing a boulder into place. She peeled off her bra and pants. The process felt like a full-body workout, but finally she collapsed onto her bed in the dark, letting tears silently flow until she fell into a dreamless sleep, where for a few short hours she was neither depressed nor manic. She was nothing. Not a burden or a drain, just blissful oblivion.

For a few dark, miserable days, Melissa stayed in her bed, repeating the cycle of sleeping, crying, and minimal self-care. Forced showers. Meals dropped off by Cheryl. Binge-watching Gilmore Girls or switching to Supernatural when Gilmore Girls felt too close to home. She ignored her phone, which she knew probably hurt Logan, who had messaged her many times, but she couldn't help feeling like she was doing him a favor.

Knowing she only had a few days of isolation before she'd have to drag herself to a baby shower made time feel like it was speeding up. She couldn't miss it, but she wished she could go and not be there at the same time. Putting on the facade of being okay, pretending she wasn't a waste of space, and faking happiness felt harder than deadlifting her car.

She knew her grip on sanity was slipping and that she should probably do something. What something was, was the problem. She couldn't put a finger on it, which was why isolation felt safe. If she was the problem, then removing herself at least minimized the damage.

Her logic, if spoken aloud, would have been dismantled by kind lies, so she said nothing to Cheryl, Sloan, or Logan.

When the morning arrived, she tried to think in steps. Maybe she could pick out clothes. Then eat breakfast. Then get in the car. Then out. Then into Sloan's house. These were things she'd done before and could do again, even if they felt insurmountable. Steps. That was what her therapist had suggested long ago, before Jeremy but after Rachel Moore.

She got out of bed, put on a soft sundress and sandals, and went to the kitchen. Cheryl, reading the newspaper and sipping coffee, froze mid sip when she saw her daughter willingly exit her room.

Melissa poured herself coffee and sat across from her mom. "Would you like something to eat? I bought bagels yesterday."

"That would be nice," Melissa said, her voice strained from not speaking for days.

Cheryl jumped up and put a bagel in the toaster, then set out cream cheese. When it dinged, she placed the plate in front of Melissa. "Thanks."

Cheryl tried desperately to stay casual as Melissa ate. Seeing her daughter dressed and upright without pleading gave her hope. She had already started rehearsing excuses for Melissa missing the baby shower. Melissa having caught a stomach bug. Her going would be so much better.

"When you're finished, I could braid your hair if you'd like. It looks great now," Cheryl said casually.

Melissa knew her hair was a mess and knew Cheryl was just trying to help. And for the first time since leaving Logan's apartment, she laughed. It was small but felt good.

"So does that smile mean yes?"

"Sure, Mom, you can braid my hair," Melissa said between bites.

Cheryl got so excited she immediately gathered the supplies. She barely restrained herself from starting before Melissa finished, but she waited. Melissa even made a show of her final bite. "There you go. My scalp is all yours."

Letting her mom brush her hair felt soothing. Whether it was the bristles on her scalp or her mother's fingers twisting and shaping the braid, Melissa wasn't sure. Cheryl had braided her hair for holidays and special occasions when she was younger. As she grew older, she declined more often than not. The last time she'd agreed was graduation.

When Cheryl tied off the braid, calm washed over Melissa. She was dressed. She was groomed. She had eaten. Three solid steps.

Cheryl kissed the top of her head. "I'm going to grab the blanket and my purse. We should leave in a few minutes. Are you ready?"

"Yes," Melissa said.

Chapter 20: Baby Mama

"Maybe I shouldn't go in," Melissa said as Cheryl pulled into a parking spot in front of Sloan's house.

Cheryl turned off the engine and looked at Melissa with a gaze only a mother could give. Melissa knew there was no argument strong enough to convince her she shouldn't go inside. She had passed the point of no return.

Melissa looked out the window at a small group of women heading toward Sloan's front door. Brooke stood greeting them. It seemed so easy for her to extrovert herself. Cheryl was already at the trunk grabbing the wrapped blanket as Melissa gingerly opened her door.

Brooke waved as Melissa stood. Melissa waved back, already exhausted. Cheryl linked arms with her and guided her toward the front door and a smiling Brooke.

"Melly Mel, we're so glad you came."

"Yep. Couldn't miss Sloan's shower," Melissa said sincerely, though her thoughts spiraled about the nickname and the royal we.

After brief greetings between Cheryl and Brooke, they went inside. Sloan's house looked professionally deep cleaned and decorated. Banners and signs pointed guests to the bathroom. A wall of guessing games waited for answers. There was even a baby onesie decorating station. Melissa wondered if Brooke or Jenna had gotten an Etsy sponsorship with how much they must have spent.

She followed a sign to a table of perfectly cooked appetizers and specialty mocktails with names like Berry Sweet Baby and Mama Mosa. Cheryl had left to drop off the blanket at the gift table, so Melissa didn't notice Sloan beside her until she spoke.

"I know it's a bit obnoxious. It was mostly Jenna. Brooke didn't rein her in or anything. I guess I didn't either."

"Hey you," Melissa said after a moment. "This is very, I don't know, I couldn't have pulled this off. Look, you have three signature mocktails. I'm going with the Preggy Punch. Probably the worst name of the lot, but I do like a carbonated punch."

"I'm so glad you're here for this," Sloan said, grabbing Melissa's empty hand and locking eyes with her. The eye contact made Melissa want to cry, and she wasn't sure why. Sloan looked more pregnant than Melissa remembered, maybe because the maternity dress was designed to show it off. Either way, Sloan glowed. "Come grab a seat next to me."

Sloan guided her to the couch. They watched guests mingle. Melissa suspected Jenna and Brooke had stacked the party with their wealthier friends, which meant Sloan would get everything on her registry and then some. It was probably for the best. Even at her best, Melissa wouldn't have thought to invite people like this.

Cheryl finally returned after chatting with others.

"Your place looks great. You look so beautiful," Cheryl said as she hugged Sloan. Then she sat in a chair next to

Melissa, which was a relief until Melissa wondered if that, too, had been planned.

"I'm sure I'm going to turn into a balloon. This kiddo is already tap dancing on my bladder," Sloan said, deflecting the compliment.

"Well, that's what you get for staying hydrated," Melissa said reflexively, surprising herself.

"You're right. I should become a desert wasteland and really make this kid work for nutrients. The real world starts in utero, kid, buckle up," Sloan said, rubbing her belly lovingly.

They bantered gently while Cheryl left to grab a plate and drink. For a while, Melissa forgot how much she hadn't wanted to come.

That didn't stop Brooke from sweeping in like a cruise director.

"All right, looks like everyone who RSVP'd is here. Thanks, ladies and Todd."

"Who's Todd?" Melissa asked quietly.

"Jenna's GBF. I don't know why he calls himself that, but he came early to paint a mural for the baby's room that's gorgeous, so he gets to eat and drink whatever he wants," Sloan said, waving at Todd. He wore a paint splattered onesie, hair perfectly coiffed.

The group gathered around Sloan. Melissa wondered if she was sitting in the middle of a fire hazard.

Brooke stood in front of Sloan, which meant Melissa's view was entirely Brooke's ass. She pretended to clink her glass. Melissa slumped lower.

"I hope everyone's enjoying the snacks and drinks. Thank you for coming today to celebrate my sister Sloan's baby shower. It means so much to us. And pardon the sappy moment, but I just want to say, in front of witnesses, how proud I am of you and how happy I am for you. I love you, little sister. And I can't wait to meet this kid. To Sloan and Baby."

The room clapped and whooped. Sloan hugged her sister.

"Okay, enough sap. We're here to have fun, so put your guesses down and decorate a onesie. We'll start our toilet paper diaper tournament after Guess the Chocolate in the Diaper. Jenna, can you help me?"

Before Melissa could ask why anyone should sniff melted chocolate bars in diapers, she had a Twix diaper shoved in her hand. She reluctantly played. With every diaper passed, her will to live dwindled. She tried to escape multiple times, but Sloan always grabbed her knee.

After the tenth and final diaper, which Melissa guessed was Almond Joy, the game ended.

Unfortunately, the Toilet Paper Diaper game followed. Teams of two, rolls of toilet paper, and tape. One person built the diaper on their teammate, and Sloan judged.

Melissa and Cheryl teamed up. Melissa built. Every unraveling of toilet paper felt like labor without reward.

As Cheryl modeled Melissa's sad excuse for a diaper, Melissa watched the other teams laughing. Maybe she should have stayed home. This party only seemed to be getting worse for her.

As if Sloan sensed it, she herded Melissa back to the couch. A glance at her watch showed only two hours had passed. Melissa could have sworn it was all day.

"Congrats to Todd and Jenna on the best diaper. Looks like Sloan should hit you two up if she has diaper issues," Brooke announced as Todd continued posing in toilet paper.

Melissa rolled her eyes.

"Now we're going to watch the mommy of honor open her gifts, so let's all settle."

Melissa was relieved the games were over, but the idea of performing delight at someone else opening gifts, even Sloan, felt exhausting. She tried to diagnose why. It wasn't jealousy. Watching people open gifts was boring. The fun part was giving or receiving. If you weren't doing either, why be part of the moment?

She imagined giving a sarcastic monologue about the ritual, but exhaustion pinned her to the couch as wrapping paper flew. Cards about motherhood and blessings blurred together into a shapeless monologue punctuated by oohs and ahhs.

Then Cheryl's blanket was unwrapped.

Sloan pulled out the massive aquamarine blanket and immediately rubbed it on her face. "Oh my god, Cheryl, this is so beautiful. It's so soft. I love it. The baby will too. Thank you."

More oohs and ahhs. Happy tears welled as Sloan and Cheryl hugged. Sloan hugged Melissa too, but Melissa felt hollow. She hadn't helped make the blanket or bought yarn. She had done nothing. She wished she had stayed in bed and let Cheryl say she was sick. She was sick. Sick and tired of pretending.

She knew it was garbage to feel this way, but she didn't have the strength to lie to everyone else or herself.

As gifts wrapped up, people began saying goodbye. Melissa felt her social battery drain completely and slipped away while Sloan was distracted. Cheryl was in the kitchen insisting on helping Jenna and Brooke clean, so Melissa picked up trash in the living room. After all, she was trash, so she might as well put herself where she belonged.

"Thank you again, Todd. That mural with the sleepy moon is beautiful," Sloan said as Todd said goodbye. Soon, it was just Sloan and Melissa in the living room. Gentle clinking and laughter came from the kitchen.

Sloan watched Melissa.

She had tried all day to make Melissa feel wanted. Included. She kept asking herself why her friend couldn't see it. Sloan had done understanding, kind, and concerned. What else was left? Watching someone you love drown is brutal, especially when you can see paths out that they refuse to take.

She decided to try again.

"Hey, you," Sloan said.

"I thought I'd help. Sorry," Melissa said, stuffing trash into the bag.

Sloan dropped a cup in. "You don't have to do that. It's your party"

"What is happening here? I'm really confused," Sloan said softly.

Melissa shrugged.

Something snapped in Sloan. "You look like you haven't slept in days. You stopped texting me. I didn't even know if you were coming today."

"I'm trying to get my shit together like you told me to," Melissa snapped, baffled at being grilled when she'd shown up, participated, drank the overly sugary punch, and helped clean.

"This doesn't look like that. Can you honestly say this is what getting your shit together looks like?" Sloan said, pulling the garbage bag away.

Melissa stared at her.

"Oh, so you get pregnant and now you want to parent me?" Melissa shot back.

"Jesus, that is not what I'm doing," Sloan said, hurt.

"Really? You didn't involve me in throwing the baby shower," Melissa said.

"I thought you had enough going on," Sloan said defensively.

"I HAVE NOTHING GOING ON," Melissa screamed. The noise in the kitchen stopped. Sloan stepped back. "Sorry my issues are getting in the way of your perfect life."

Cheryl, Jenna, and Brooke stood frozen in the doorway.

"Your issues are all you think about. You're acting like a child. You can't be trusted to throw a shower. You couldn't be trusted to come to one without your mom. My needs mean nothing to you," Sloan said. "I'm going to be a mother. That means protecting this for the rest of my life. This is huge. And you've barely acknowledged it. The only time you seemed to care was when I asked you to be a godparent. Shocking, you only care when it's about you."

"Maybe you should make Jenna the godparent then. Or Todd. He seems great with DIY projects," Melissa said, wishing she had something better.

"Right now, Todd has done more for this baby than you have. Maybe he should be the godmother," Sloan snapped. "You've been my friend for over a decade and you're treating me like I bailed on you, when you're the one bailing on me."

"I'm sorry I'm a mess," Melissa said. She had nothing left but defeat. Everyone knew she was broken. There was no hiding anymore.

"We're all messes. That's life. You're hurting me, your mom, yourself, and you're actively hurting others. Who do you think you are?" Sloan asked. "Rachel Moore hurt you as a child. She is not the problem. You still haven't dealt with what Jeremy did. He was the asshole. He hurt you."

"No, he loved me. He was supposed to be safe. I just wasn't enough," Melissa said, tears welling.

Cheryl moved toward her, but Sloan held up a hand.

"No, he didn't. If he had, he wouldn't have knocked up someone else," Sloan said flatly.

Melissa broke. Tears streamed down her face.

"Right. And who could love someone like me, right?" she said.

"No. I'm not doing this. I'm done. It's not good for the baby. Melissa, I love you, but I can't. You need help. Professional help," Sloan said.

Melissa staggered back against the wall.

Cheryl rushed to her. "Honey, Sloan is right. Maybe it's time to talk to Dr. David again. You aren't yourself."

The words felt like gut punches.

"I know you and I aren't close," Brooke said, stepping forward, "but my sister loves you as much as she loves me. So don't ignore what she or your sweetheart of a mom is saying."

Then Brooke followed Sloan down the hall.

Melissa couldn't meet anyone's eyes.

"If you want, we can call now and book an appointment. Together," Cheryl said softly, pulling out her phone. "I have his number saved"

That sentence was a starter pistol.

Melissa bolted.

She ran from the house, skin crawling with panic and self-hatred. She didn't know where she was going, only that staying wasn't an option. She needed distance. As much as she could get.

Chapter 21: Employee of the Month

Dramatically running away from your problems rarely fixes them, which was the lesson Melissa learned in this moment. Cardio had never been her thing, and after a short, humiliating run, she wondered if she should just take a Lyft home. But once she slowed to a walk, she kept going until she found herself in front of Stone's Throw Grocery. She wasn't sure if it was intentional or instinct, but it felt safe.

Melissa walked inside and spotted Logan checking out a customer. He didn't notice her at first, but something must have clicked because he looked up and locked eyes with her. He understood immediately that something was wrong, but he had to finish with the customer. He lifted a finger apologetically, asking for a second.

She nodded and drifted toward a shelf of small houseplants.

"Thank you for coming to Stone's Throw. Have a wonderful day," Logan said, wrapping up quickly. The second the customer pushed their cart away, Logan speed walked over.

"Hey, where have you been? You totally ghosted me after"

Melissa combusted, crying the same way she had at Sloan's house. Logan pulled her into a hug without hesitation, confusion and concern washing over him. She stayed there until she could speak.

"I told you I'm a mess. I just had a huge fight with everyone. I don't know what's wrong with me. You're the only one who seems to like me. I can't figure out why."

"Hey, hey," Logan said. "I don't dispassionately make out with hungover people in my apartment after cooking them breakfast if I don't like them. That would be a terrible policy."

"You're so lovely. Can you name one screwed up thing about yourself? I feel like Prince Charming is trying to date a swamp creature," Melissa pleaded.

Logan laughed. "Well, my penis is only average sized."

Melissa snorted, then cried harder.

He wiped her tears and thought more seriously. "I usually don't list flaws before date three, but I rarely put dirty clothes in the hamper. I have hampers. I just use the floor. I paint Warhammer 40,000 figures, specifically Necrons, and I'm in an online DnD campaign that started in 2020."

"Those are quirks. Give me something I can work with," Melissa said, almost joking.

"I'm missing my appendix, so I have a scar, and most of my left pinky toe is gone."

Her eyes widened.

"There was an accident. I'm klutzy. I was playing DnD, sitting at my computer, drinking Hawaiian Punch mixed with Sprite. I'm a half elf rogue, which isn't important, but still. I rolled the dice and one fell off my desk. I dove for it. I must have hit the table leg and it snapped off and landed on my bare toe, completely smashing it. Doctors saved what they could, but it turns out it's easier to smash a toe than unsmash one."

"So you have nine toes?" Melissa asked.

"Nine and a half. I got lucky. Only the pinky went. But imagine if it hit my head. I can live without a toe, maybe even a foot, but yeah. Good enough flaw?"

"A missing toe is the worst thing about you?"

"I'm not sure what has to be wrong with me to make liking you make sense," Logan said honestly.

"I don't know either," Melissa said.

"Sorry I'm apparently perfect and still like you."

"Shut up," Melissa said, smacking his arm lightly. "Do you still want a date for your friend's wedding tomorrow?"

Logan paused, letting her sweat for half a second. "I'd be honored to bring a swamp creature to a wedding."

Melissa grimaced. She'd earned that one.

She sweet talked Logan into dropping her home on his break. When they pulled up, she saw Cheryl inside watching her new obsession, Yellowstone. Melissa kissed Logan quickly and stepped out, but he didn't drive away until she was halfway up the path.

She rolled her eyes. Some dumb chivalry thing. Still, now she had to face her mom.

Inside, Cheryl didn't react. Melissa expected something, anything, but Cheryl kept watching TV. Melissa went to the kitchen for water, making enough noise to be noticed. Still nothing.

"I'm home," Melissa said.

Cheryl lifted a hand without turning. "Do you want to talk about what happened at the shower?"

"Do you?" Cheryl asked flatly.

Melissa froze. This was not what she'd expected. She would have bet everything Cheryl would be frantic, demanding details. Instead, Cheryl barely looked at her.

"I guess not," Melissa said, panic rising. Had she broken her mom? Did Cheryl hate her now?

"Okay. Goodnight," Cheryl said, eyes still on the TV.

Melissa considered turning off the television and demanding attention but couldn't bring herself to. Had she hurt her mom by leaving the shower like that? Sloan had said she hurt people without noticing. Maybe she had.

Choosing the path of least resistance, she went to her room, serenaded by explosions from Yellowstone.

She closed the door and looked around. She'd dreamed all day of being alone in this room. Now it felt wrong. She stripped off her dress and wiped her face with a makeup remover pad, replaying the day.

Then one thought bulldozed everything else.

Tomorrow, she would finally have a shot at Rachel Moore.

She could fix karma, then fix everything else. Balance the universe and move forward. Everyone could cool off. Maybe they'd realize she didn't need therapy. Things would be fine in forty eight hours. She'd lived with discomfort for months. A few more days wouldn't kill her.

Melissa pulled on Logan's white shirt and climbed into bed.

After today, nothing would be harder than self destructing in front of everyone you loved. Which meant the only direction left was up.

With that thought, she fell into a deep, dreamless sleep.

Chapter 22: The Wedding Date

Waking up in her bed for the first time with purpose was an exhilarating feeling. Sure, she had forced herself to occasionally DoorDash or go to a disastrous party, but today was the day she could right a twenty year old wrong. That was not the type of thing that happened every day, she thought to herself in a self gratified manner. To kick off the celebration, the first thing she did was text Logan. She felt like she owed him so much, but she kept it simple with a "Good morning, can't wait to go to the wedding!"

Satisfied that she was going to absolutely smash today, she sat up and thought about what she was going to wear. She decided that she would first make herself a cup of coffee and gauge Cheryl's feelings about yesterday. However, when Melissa poked her head out of her room and gingerly walked into the kitchen, she was surprised to see that the house was empty. There was no coffee in the pot or any of the room's usual warmth.

She continued to make herself something to eat as she brewed coffee, but the emptiness of the house did put a small strain on her happy morning. The crunch of her cinnamon toast seemed to echo when she bit into it, and she walked back to her room. Melissa checked her phone, unable to refocus on the wedding. Besides a text from Logan sending an assortment of emojis in response to her message, there was nothing. No missed texts or calls.

As she started going through her dress options, her mind kept wandering to her mother's absence. Where was Cheryl? Why hadn't she told Melissa she was not going to be home. Was this some kind of parental punishment thing? It was between these trains of thought that Melissa selected a blue dress that really made her boobs look massive. She figured that would at minimum make Logan happy. She continued going through the motions of doing her hair and makeup, refusing to dwell on her mom or Sloan. That was for tomorrow. After she finished what needed to be done, she could fix everything.

Melissa's hardest conundrum was her purse. While she had a small clutch that would have gone with the dress, the problem was that it was too small. She needed to bring her fancy camera with high resolution and fast shutter speeds. Using her camera guaranteed she would get a high quality photo of Rachel in the act of cheating without the risk of blur. So she went with a small leather backpack. It just barely fit her camera, phone, ID, credit card, and lip gloss, but it got the job done without having to bring something outrageous like a canvas backpack that would definitely make her stand out.

When Logan pulled up in his Toyota 4Runner, he hopped out to open the door for Melissa. She could not help but enjoy the moment. It almost felt like a real date and not a mission of revenge. Logan even held her hand as they drove to the Ritz Carlton. They talked about how excited his friend was about getting married.

Ezra Cohen and Logan had been friends since high school. Apparently they bonded through their mutual love of tabletop gaming and comic books. Their biggest fight was over who was the better comic writer, Ed Brubaker or Neil Gaiman, which had led to a full month of radio silence during college. However, it was Gracie Kamaka who had convinced Ezra that this was the dumbest thing she had ever heard and told him to make up with Logan. Apparently this was how she won all the hearts of Ezra's friends, since the rift between him and Logan had stalled a DnD game, and their reconciliation led to the successful completion of the campaign. This story filled the entire car ride, and when they got to the hall, Logan made her wait so he could open the door again for her. He handed the keys to a valet, then held out his arm to walk Melissa into the Ritz like a gentleman.

The room had been meticulously decorated in white hibiscus and pink plumerias, making it smell like Hawaii had somehow been planted indoors. There was a photo sign of the happy couple stating that this was the Cohen Kamaka wedding. The soft glow coming in through the windows made everything feel warm. Everything was soft and perfect and reeked of money. Melissa suddenly wondered how much money Logan and his friends actually had as Logan sat her down in a seat.

"I'm really sorry, I just have to go make sure the groom isn't doing anything stupid. I couldn't be the best man due to family stuff, but I'm sort of like the hand of the king," Logan said before kissing her quickly. "I'll be back."

Melissa watched Logan walk up the aisle to look for Ezra. He breezed down the pathway, occasionally stopped for a quick handshake or wave. He was so at ease as he social-butterflied his way into a side door. Melissa hoped he would do something wrong on his way back. Why was it so effortless for him?

"He doesn't have all his toes," Melissa said out loud, reminding herself that he was not perfect. "Plus he's a nerd. A big old nerd."

"Sounds like you're talking about Logan," said a friendly guy in a sleek tuxedo and yarmulke. He looked like a more rugged version of the groom, with a thick short beard and tan skin. Where Ezra had no beard and a translucent quality. "I'm Adam, the groom's older brother. You must be vomit girl."

"Oh god," Melissa muttered, horrified. This did not seem to phase Adam. On the contrary, he was delighted that this made her uncomfortable. However, like a hero, Logan reappeared by her side.

"Whoa now, I don't trust you chatting with Melissa alone. You tend to," Logan drew out his thoughts, "be a total ass."

They both laughed and hugged. Adam explained that he was just introducing himself and that he was on his way to be by Ezra's side. Logan gestured for him to get to it, then reclaimed his seat beside Melissa. Melissa wrapped her arms around his arm, the way a child would hug a stuffed animal. There they stayed until the wedding began. A live pianist and cello started playing Canon in D as Ezra walked to stand by the rabbi. Melissa could not help thinking how beautiful it sounded, but Logan's whispering commentary about who was who in the bridal party kept her from crying.

Everything was so beautiful that it set Melissa's body on fire. She was so happy to be sitting in this room with

Logan, watching two people have a fairy tale. It was strange, but it almost felt like she was watching some cinematic conclusion. The groom looked perfectly groomed in the crispiest black tuxedo she had ever seen. When the bride made her appearance, Melissa was gobsmacked. Gracie's ivory dress had a sweetheart neckline that accentuated her natural beauty, with a delicate floral tulle overlay that matched her bouquet. A dainty veil popped against her thick dark hair. She was both whimsical and ethereal, a bride you would kill to be.

The bride and groom both began to tear up as they shared vows, I dos, and the kiss. The whole room erupted in cheers as Ezra broke a glass with his foot. And just like that, they were married. The only time Logan broke free from her grip was when he gleefully cheered for his friend. Realizing his mistake, he quickly offered his arm again but could not stop clapping. Melissa found it endearing that he could not stop being happy for his friend but also did not want her to think she had been forgotten. The crowd was introduced to Mr and Mrs Cohen and asked to move into another room for cocktail hour.

As the crowd began to move, Melissa slowly slipped out of wedding mode and into revenge mode. Logan did not seem to notice her starting to clutch her bag, reconfirming that her camera was still inside. Or that she did not go too deeply into the room, staying close to the door so she could see the front desk. If she stayed there, she would see the exact moment Rachel arrived.

"You should try these. I think they're cranberry fig goat cheese crostini," Logan said, trying to hand her one. She shook her head no, breaking eye contact with the front desk for a moment. "You should eat a little something. I think I saw artichoke phyllo cups. They looked good."

"I don't want to miss seeing her," Melissa said, not feeling hungry in the slightest. Logan sighed to himself. A part of him had hoped Melissa would be having so much fun she would forget about Rachel. He had not succeeded. Worse, he felt her growing more distant and it made him uncomfortable.

"Aye, oh, Logan and vomit girl," Adam said as he came up with a plate of tequila shots. Logan gave him a look and Adam rolled his eyes. "I come bearing drinks. I'm sorry, Melissa. Drink."

"Oh, I think we should probably wait til," Logan began, but Melissa unconsciously took a shot. Logan shrugged and took one with Adam. "I guess we're not waiting for dinner. Hey, Ezra."

Ezra came over and pulled Logan into a hug, then noticed Melissa, who was still distracted. Logan gripped her hand, silently pleading for her attention. "Melissa, I'd love you to meet my best friend, Ezra."

"This is the famous Melissa?" Ezra asked, pulling her into a hug and dragging her eyes away from the desk. Melissa pulled out of it, confused. "It's great to meet you. This guy's losing his shit over you, I hope you know."

"What. Oh. Thanks?" Melissa said, trying to blink herself into the present while her brain screamed at her to look back at the front desk. What if she missed Rachel. The guys kept talking, but just as Melissa was distracted by the desk, Logan was distracted by Melissa. Suddenly, Rachel Moore walked into the room wearing a trench coat and dark thick glasses. Melissa grabbed her camera and started taking photos. Logan thought she was photographing him and his friends until he realized she was focused on the front desk.

"I have to go," Melissa said, then bolted out of the room to get closer without being seen. If anyone had been paying attention, she would have stuck out like a sore thumb. Her saving grace was that nobody cared about a random white woman from a wedding party taking photos. Logan watched her and for the first time wondered if Melissa was not okay. He knew she had things to work through, but this moment made him wonder if it was beyond his abilities.

"Your girl is real weird, bro," Adam said before offering another round of shots. Logan took one with his friends and decided he was not out yet. He had invited her under the impression that he would help her. However, a thought crept into the front of his mind that he dreaded. Was he just being used.

"Melissa's great. Just a little distracted. I'm going to go check on her," Logan said firmly before leaving cocktail hour. As he exited the room, he saw Melissa approaching the front desk attendant. They were mid conversation when Logan reached her.

Chapter 23: It's Complicated

Melissa had watched Rachel turn a corner toward the elevators, where a man in a hoodie had been waiting for her. She had snapped a photo but only caught the back of his sweater and Rachel's coat. So she concluded her only shot was getting to the room. The front desk attendant was not going to make it easy, even after polite pleasantries and explaining she knew Rachel. The company line was firm.

"I cannot give out personal information about our guests."

"That was Rachel Moore. I've known her for a long time. I'd love to send her a bottle of champagne or something. Could you tell me her room number?" Melissa said with a light pleading smile.

"Miss, I don't think I can do that. That goes against our policy. I hope you understand," the front desk attendant said with finality. Melissa looked behind her and saw Logan standing a few steps back, and an idea popped into her head.

"What if I bought the bottle and gave it to you or a bellhop? They could take it up. You wouldn't need to tell me anything," Melissa offered, smiling. The front desk attendant considered it, then shrugged.

"It's an odd request, but I believe that is doable."

Melissa, elated, turned and grabbed Logan's wrist, pulling him back into the cocktail room. It was loud, and nobody paid attention as she dragged him toward the bar.

"You were really rude to my friends back there," Logan said, trying to slow her down, but Melissa did not have slow in her.

"I promise I will make it up to them, but our plan is a go, so we need to move fast," Melissa said as she spotted an unopened bottle of champagne. She looked around, making sure no one besides Logan was watching, then swiped it. To be fair, if anyone cared about this kind of theft, Melissa would have been caught immediately. It was an open bar. If she had asked, the bartender would have given it to her without question. That fact did not seem to occur to Melissa as she scampered from the room.

"Okay, I'm going to give this to the front desk attendant, who will take it to Rachel Moore. You just need to follow the bottle and tell me what room it goes to," Melissa said, holding it up. When Logan did not look as enthused as she hoped, she continued. "I'll go knock on the door, snap a couple shots, then bam. Done. I'll send them to Mr Moore and call it karma completed. Then we can get back to the wedding."

"Let me head toward the elevators first. I'll wait there and see where it goes," Logan said reluctantly before leaving. Melissa took a moment to steady herself, her head finally turning to really look at the party. She could understand why Logan wanted to stay instead of following her revenge plan, but he was only needed for this step. Then he could go back to his life. Maybe this would be the final straw for them, but at least she would have her revenge. That thought sobered her for a moment.

She handed the bottle to the front desk attendant, then went back to stand near the party door, thinking about how she had pushed everyone away. Sloan, her mom, and now maybe even Logan. She would get revenge, but what if the damage she caused to get it was too much. What if she ended up with no one. Without realizing it, tears started trickling down her face.

"You okay?" Adam asked, appearing again with a fresh tray of shots. Melissa looked at him and suddenly he reminded her of Jeremy. Not because they looked alike, but because of how easily they found her at her weakest moments. Unlike Jeremy, Adam actually seemed concerned. "I'm going to need a little confirmation here. You all right. Did something happen."

"No, I'm fine," Melissa said, then took a shot as proof. Adam seemed to accept this form of confirmation and shrugged.

"You're one of those cry at weddings girls. Got it," Adam said, heading back into the party.

Melissa touched her face and felt tears for the first time. She wiped at them, but that only made her mascara smudge. She kept wiping, not realizing she was making her appearance match her mental state.

Logan finally returned from the elevators and walked over to her. The relief she felt was enormous, but the same could not be said for him. He looked at her smudged face and knew she had cried while he was gone. He did not like feeling like part of this anymore.

"Oh thank god. Did you get the number?" Melissa asked.

"1504. Are you sure you want to do this? We could just go back to the party together," Logan said, and he wondered if she could hear the pleading in his voice. Melissa, however, felt nothing but elation at the room number. She was so close to finishing this.

"If you were being cheated on, wouldn't you want someone to tell you? Wouldn't you want someone, even a stranger, to care enough to give you a heads up?" Melissa asked, oblivious to what Logan needed in the moment. Logan shrugged, half yes, but when she turned toward the elevators, he stopped her.

"What."

"You'll need this. I swiped it from the delivery guy. It should get you into the room," Logan said, handing her a keycard. He knew she would do something reckless if he did not help, but he hated himself for giving it to her. Still, he tried again. "Look, I know I said I was okay with this, but maybe this is too far for me. I really like you. I wanted us to have a fun night. This is not fun for me. If you go up there, no matter what, someone gets hurt. That's on you and me now because I helped you. And that doesn't feel good."

Logan swallowed hard and looked down at his feet. Melissa blinked as more tears slid silently down her face, dragging mascara with them. She had done it. She had pushed everyone away. Now all she had left was Rachel Moore.

"The only person who's going to get hurt is Rachel Moore. Just desserts for an asshole," Melissa said. Logan nodded knowingly.

"I should have known. Why on earth would someone like you actually be into me? I bet I was some kind of She's All That challenge. I don't even wear glasses."

"I don't get that reference, but I just liked you," Logan said, then could not stop himself from being a little petty. "You're the reason this isn't happening. It's on you. I was fully in. Good luck with everything. I hope you get what you're looking for."

Logan walked back into the party, defeated. Melissa turned toward the elevators and pressed the button. The doors opened and she stepped inside. White noise screamed in her ears. She was alone. She had no one. Melissa pressed fifteen and scanned the card, her heart pounding so loudly she could hear it. The elevator felt like it was rocketing upward and moving at a glacial pace at the same time. How could both be true, she thought.

"Get it together. Get it together," Melissa said as she pulled out her camera, checking the SD card, battery, and lens cap. She triple checked the settings. The elevator dinged and the doors slid open. "You can do this. Don't be a coward."

Melissa stepped out and followed the signs toward room 1504. It felt like she was levitating down the hall. The white walls and geometric carpet slid past her like a dream, but this was not a dream. She had pinched herself hard to confirm it. Melissa stopped in front of the door with gold numbers reading 1504 and did one final check to make sure her camera was on.

Melissa took a deep breath, used the keycard, pushed open the door, and started snapping photos without letting her feet move. She stayed outside the room, Sloan's voice in her head telling her to stay put. Rachel Moore and a man were partially clothed and kissing on the bed. When the door flew open, they froze for a split second before realizing what was happening. Then they scrambled to cover themselves, flashes from the camera making them shield their eyes. The man tripped while trying to pull on his pants.

"Enjoying your affair, you cheater? Is no one safe?" Melissa yelled.

"Moppy? I'm not cheating, this is my husband, you fucking psycho," Rachel shouted, lunging toward the door without caring that her body was visible.

"Yeah, sure, and I'm Kelly Clarkson," Melissa yelled back, slamming the door before running toward the elevators and hammering the button. She saw the half naked man from 1504 charging down the hall and bolted for the stairs. Melissa kicked off her heels. "Fucking heels."

She ran down the stairwell, panic coursing through her body, adrenaline steering her movements. When she hit the ground floor after fifteen flights, she saw security heading toward the stairs through a window. Melissa bolted through an emergency exit and set off an alarm.

She ran down the Ritz alleyway barefoot, then down the street. The sun had just set and streetlights were flickering on. She spotted a park across the street and made a beeline for it, convinced security was close behind her. But after running through the park and tripping into a patch of mud, she realized no one was following her. She pulled herself up and started laughing.

She was covered in mud, shoeless, in a dark park with no one who loved her, but she got the photos. She had done it. Not gracefully or skillfully, but she pulled it off. She called a Lyft to pick her up. Normally waiting alone in a dark park without shoes and covered in mud would be concerning, but tonight it did not even register.

The Lyft driver was not pleased with her appearance and pulled out a towel for her to sit on, but she was on her way home. The hard part was over. She could download the photos, write a sympathetic note to Mr. Moore, and do a grand apology tour with Sloan, her mom, and Logan. She could honestly say she would never carry out a revenge plot again. Then everyone, including her, could move on and be free.

The house lights glowed as the Lyft pulled up. Melissa grabbed her things and went inside. As she walked, she left bloody footprints from cuts she had not noticed while running barefoot through stairwells, streets, and parks. She had forgotten her dress was sweat stained, ripped, and dirty, and that her face was streaked with mascara. As she did this visual self check, she forgot about the gnome. She clipped it with her foot, sending it toppling onto the concrete path where it split clean in half.

Good, she thought. I truly hated that thing.

She didn't stop. She didn't look back.

Cheryl, who had planned on continuing the silent treatment, was undone when she saw her daughter walk in. She rushed toward Melissa and accidentally knocked a plate of dinner to the floor.

"What happened?" Cheryl said, grabbing her and checking for injuries. Melissa, who had missed her mom all day, suddenly noticed how horrible she looked and felt repulsed.

"I don't want to talk about it. I'm going to shower and go to bed," Melissa said dismissively. She needed to make up with her mom when she was clean. This was not how tonight was supposed to go. As Melissa headed to the bathroom, Cheryl followed.

"Can we please talk in the morning?"

"I can't do this anymore," Cheryl said, exasperated, her eyes filling with tears. She was frightened for her daughter and no longer knew what to do. "Sloan's right, honey. If you won't see Dr David, you can't stay here. You can stay tonight. Clean up and pack, but tomorrow morning you need to leave. I can't keep watching this. I love you too much."

Melissa's tears came rushing back. She could not believe what she was hearing. She knew her mom was upset, but she had been certain things could be fixed. "Really, Mom? You too? Where am I supposed to go?"

"I don't know what else to do, baby," Cheryl said calmly before walking to her room and gently closing the door.

Melissa ripped off her dress and went to her room, pulling out her camera and opening her laptop. She turned the camera on to review the photos she had taken. She could see Rachel's face and her partner more clearly, and horror crept through her body. She opened her Rachel folder to compare with old photos, stopping at a vacation shot and then a wedding picture.

"No no no no no no no no," was all Melissa could say as the truth stared back at her. Rachel had not lied. She had not cheated. The weight of Melissa's mistake slammed into her. She ripped the SD card from the camera and threw it. It bounced off the wall and dropped into a floor vent, disappearing into darkness.

Out of disgust, she permanently deleted the Rachel folder. She felt lower than garbage, like raw sewage sweeping into people's lives, like an overflowing septic tank in human form. Everyone had tried to warn her. Why had she not listened. Had she been self sabotaging. If so, she had succeeded. How could her life get worse. She had no one, no job, and no home.

Red and blue lights began flashing through her window. Melissa looked outside and nodded, as if agreeing with the universe. She pulled on sweatpants and a sweater when the doorbell rang. She heard Cheryl leave her room.

"Officers, you must have the wrong house. What is this about?"

Melissa slipped on socks and shoes as the officers confirmed they were at the right address and looking for Melissa Bonetti. She walked to the door herself.

There were two officers, one young and bulky, the other an older woman who looked like she took no shit from anyone. The woman spotted Melissa. "Melissa Bonetti, could you please step outside?"

"Mom, I know this doesn't mean much now, but I'm sorry. I was wrong. So wrong. And I'll see Dr David again. When I'm out of this," Melissa whispered, hugging her tightly. "I really am sorry."

Melissa stepped outside and was cuffed. As she was led to the squad car, the younger officer read her Miranda rights. She had heard them so many times on TV, but never thought they would be said to her. As she was guided into the back seat, she heard Cheryl shout.

"Do not say anything, Melissa. Nothing. I'm calling our lawyer now. You hear me? She's invoking her right to speak to her attorney."

The officers ignored her as they drove away. It was Melissa's first time in the back of a cop car. She was not a fan.

Chapter 24: Legally Blonde

When she found herself at the police station, Melissa was surprised by how calm she felt. There was no white noise, no racing heart, no dizziness. Things were bad, but maybe she had used up all her panic earlier. Her fight or flight response was off. All that remained was acceptance.

She did all the classics. Mugshot against the height chart, fingerprints, photos of her cuts and bruises. But the pièce de résistance was being placed in an interrogation room with a glass of water. Since her mother had invoked her right to counsel, questioning could not begin until her lawyer arrived. Melissa did not mind waiting. It was not like she was in a rush to sleep in a cell. The cops, however, were not thrilled about delaying their return home.

Melissa's head snapped toward the door when she heard a familiar voice from down the hall.

"I swear to god if my client's rights have been violated in any way, I will personally defund the police myself. No, I will tell you when I'm done conferring with my client."

Sloan burst into the room and locked eyes with Melissa as she closed the door behind her.

"Any recording devices or people behind that mirror better be gone," Sloan said.

They stood in silence for a moment as Sloan scanned the room before finally sitting across from Melissa. Sloan took a breath, clearly deciding what tone to take.

"Your mom knows I'm a real estate attorney, right? I mean, I know a little about criminal law, but"

"You're the only lawyer she knows or likes. To her, you're every type of lawyer. Didn't she ask you to help draft a will?"

"Yeah, she did. It's very weird that I know what your mom wants to do with her money and body, but you refuse to know," Sloan sighed, pulling paperwork from her briefcase and scanning it again while trying to build a plan. "Okay, you're going to"

"I'm sorry," Melissa said. "I know I screwed up. Not just this." She gestured at the room. "You are one of the most important people in my life. Instead of losing my mind with joy about your baby, I focused on my pain and was incredibly selfish. You deserved more. It's not an excuse. I just couldn't see through the haze. It's like living under a wet blanket. I hurt you. I will make it right somehow. I see it now. I need to get my shit together. I'm just so sorry."

Melissa word vomited herself into silence. She stumbled, lost her train of thought, and knew the speech was imperfect, but under the circumstances, she hoped it was enough. Sloan was not ready to deal with forgiveness yet. She needed to focus on her job.

"Mel, invasion of privacy is a class C felony. I'm not sure I can fix this."

"What does that mean?" Melissa asked, seeing the seriousness on Sloan's face.

"Maximum five years in prison. Depending on how much a judge wants to make an example of you," Sloan said evenly, though concern leaked through. Melissa stared at her reflection in the two way mirror, still a mess in every way. The anti Mary Poppins. Sloan placed her hand over Melissa's, grounding her. "You don't have a record, so I think we can get this pleaded down to probation, but you'd still be a felon. I can ask around about getting someone with real criminal experience"

"Oh my god, I'm going to be sick. I didn't go into the room. I stayed in the hallway. Five years for standing in a hallway," Melissa said, scanning for a trash can. Sloan pulled a barf bag from her purse.

"I had morning sickness at the office, so I keep these around," Sloan said, handing it to her. "Listen, being a felon isn't great, but it beats prison. No offense, but you are not built for that."

Melissa scoffed, and despite everything, it felt good to have her friend on her side again. A hard knock sounded at the door.

"Excuse you, I am speaking with my client," Sloan snapped as she stood and opened it.

"I come bearing good news," said a haggard man in his sixties. He walked in with a file and took Sloan's seat while Sloan stood behind Melissa. "Miss Bonetti, I'm Detective Martinez. And you're an idiot."

"Excuse me? Can I get your badge number? This is," Sloan began, already furious, but the detective did not seem to care.

"Your client didn't put an SD card in the camera. No photos," he said, giving Melissa a suspicious look. They had already searched her, so he knew she did not have one. He was half hoping she would confess out of outrage at being called an idiot. Melissa said nothing.

Sloan lit up. "Hold on. Trespassing isn't a felony. She didn't even go into the room. At best, the hotel would have to press charges, and I doubt they want to advertise that a stranger easily accessed a luxury hotel room."

"You wouldn't be wrong," Detective Martinez said, flipping open his file and pushing it toward them. "Your slip up was your luckiest move. So as a participation prize, you get two things."

"What is this?" Sloan asked, picking up the paperwork.

"One, a lifetime ban from Ritz Carlton. Two, a restraining order. You must stay at least five hundred feet away from Rachel and Connor Moore at all times. Do you understand?"

"I will avoid her and that hotel at all costs," Melissa said.

"These are standard orders, but I will review them with my client to ensure she understands the gravity of the situation," Sloan said.

"Her freedom depends on it. Hope you have a good night. You're free to leave," Detective Martinez said, standing and walking out.

Once he was gone, Sloan grabbed Melissa and hauled her up. Melissa had not realized her foot had fallen asleep, but she limped after Sloan anyway as they hurried out of the station.

Outside, they sprinted to Sloan's car. Once inside, Sloan finally spoke.

"Oh my god, you are so lucky. I cannot believe you forgot the SD card in that stupid camera."

"I think I know where it is. I threw it when I realized Rachel was with her husband," Melissa admitted. Sloan's jaw dropped as she started the car.

"Jesus. There was a card? As your friend, you need to destroy that thing. As your lawyer, I never heard you say shit about it."

"I feel like if I had murdered Rachel, they would have looked harder for evidence. I think they were more annoyed dealing with me than anything else," Melissa said, then both of them started laughing hysterically with relief.

When the laughter died down, Sloan grew serious.

"Your mom told me you're starting back up with Dr David. Is that real?" Sloan asked. A big part of her was afraid to hear the answer. If Melissa refused help again, Sloan knew she would have to step away. She had to protect her baby from chaos.

"I am. I haven't made the appointment yet because the police kind of delayed the call, but I can't do this to myself anymore. Or to you or my mom. I need to be better. And to quote you, get my shit together."

"Oh, your mom already made the appointment. Therapists move fast when the phrase just picked up by the cops is used," Sloan said, smiling through wet eyes.

"I guess that's fair. I haven't exactly been trustworthy lately," Melissa said, rolling her eyes at herself.

They rode in silence while Sloan put on a murder mystery podcast called Buried Bones. It was not Melissa's first choice, but it felt good just being in the same space as her friend, even if that meant listening to an eighteenth-century murder.

When Sloan pulled up to Cheryl's house, Melissa paused before opening the door. She knew her mom was awake, and she had no idea what she could say to fix everything. Sloan sensed it and pulled her into an awkward hug over the center console and pregnant belly.

"You need to get out. I'm tired and want to go home."

Melissa nodded and got out. She waved as the car drove away, then turned to face the house. It had barely taken two seconds after opening the door before Cheryl pulled her into a crushing hug. Melissa froze, then melted into it, closing the door behind her.

"You have an appointment with Dr David tomorrow," Cheryl said gently. Melissa nodded. Cheryl lifted her face and said, "If you ever bring cops to my door again, it better be because you were arrested protesting something important, like a pipeline. Understood?"

"How about I just don't get arrested anymore," Melissa said.

"I suppose that works too," Cheryl replied, then her mom brain kicked back in. "Are you hungry? I can heat up some soup."

Chapter 25: Silver Linings Playbook

Melissa had started her day with a breakdown from Cheryl about how things would be different. She was now expected to cook dinner twice a week and pitch in with chores. She didn't want to say it, but it felt like she got off lightly with these two demands from her mom. Still, she figured Cheryl was worried about pushing her too hard.

However, Cheryl also insisted on bringing Melissa to her first session with Dr. David. Sitting in his waiting room felt less daunting with her mom holding her hand as she blankly stared at a black and white photo of a bonsai tree. When her name was called, she had a flash of panic where, if her mom hadn't been there, she could see herself running. But she knew that was wrong. Her instincts were obviously not to be trusted right now.

Instead of running, she let go of her mom's hand and stood up to go into the room. Dr. David's friendly weathered face greeted her warmly as he gestured toward a dark beige couch that faced his ergonomic lounge chair and black and white artsy posters of calm images and sayings like "Be Kind to Your Mind," "Your Feelings and Needs Matter," and "It's okay to not be okay." Melissa thought the posters were stupid, but she knew Dr. David meant every word on them, which made her able to not be sassy about their existence.

"I know what your mother told me over the phone, but why don't you tell me why you've come back to therapy?" Dr. David said as he sat across from her. His face never hinted at judgment, only curiosity. This was a huge moment for

Melissa. She knew she could lie or try to make herself not sound all that bad, but what was the point?

"Well, I've been hurting a lot of people. Myself included. I pushed people away, broke some laws, basically I'm spiraling," Melissa confessed.

"Committed crimes? Well, I suppose that explains why you had yourself an adventure with our local law enforcement. Do you want to elaborate as to what exactly happened that led you to this moment?" Dr. David asked, trying to sound casual, though Melissa knew nothing about this was casual.

"Yeah, I'm not proud of how I've been acting and I don't want it to become who I am permanently. I guess I'm not really sure when it started. I mean, I know my mom thinks it was the breakup with Jeremy, but I don't know if it was," Melissa said as she bit at her cuticles subconsciously. "I knew he was an asshole, but he was my asshole. I thought he was mine. But even before the cheating, I think I was slowly losing something inside myself. Bit by bit, you know?"

"Um, I think you may have to backtrack a little. You had just started dating Jeremy when you decided to stop our sessions. You said you'd never been happier and he was your rock. He cheated?" Dr. David asked.

"Well, Jeremy didn't like that I was in therapy. He thought therapy was a waste of money and people just needed to get more vitamin D and exercise. I don't know if I actually believed it. I just wanted him to love me so much. I think I thought if I could just put the depression in a box in the back of my mind and keep distracting myself, I could… I don't know. Not need it?" Melissa said as tears began flowing down her face. She hated how often she found herself crying. She wasn't weak, her eyes just didn't want to cooperate with her need to at least look sane. "Thinking back, I don't even know if Jeremy ever liked me."

"Did you like him?" Dr. David asked.

"What? I loved him. I wanted a family with him," Melissa said reflexively.

"I only asked because you called him an asshole and he made you suppress a part of yourself to be with him, according to what you just said. Love and like aren't mutually exclusive," Dr. David said in a calm, soothing tone. Melissa grabbed a pillow and clutched it to herself.

"I mean, who would waste like eight years on someone they didn't like?" Melissa asked, but when Dr. David didn't automatically respond, it forced her to come to terms with the truth. "I thought I did, but he was really mean. Like he didn't hit me, but he used to say things that were just borderline enough. I wasn't enough, even when I really tried to be. It was never enough. I was too this or too that, or not enough in some way. He got worse toward the end, so when he got some twenty year old blonde pregnant, I was just more surprised he didn't end things with me. Cheating I guess adds up, but why wait for me to catch him?"

"I can't answer for him definitively, but it sounds like he wanted that chaos to ensue. It caused you to do the heavy lifting in breaking up, and then he was able to drop any emotional responsibility because he had to be with this other woman. If I had to go out on a limb, I would guess he's on the spectrum of narcissism. Was it Jeremy whom you committed a crime against?"

"Oh god, no. Remember Rachel Moore?" Melissa asked with a dark scoff. Dr. David cocked his head to the side, a distant memory slowly returning.

"Rachel Moore who assaulted you in middle school?" Dr. David asked. Melissa confirmed his question with an absentminded nod. "Okay, well, it sounds like we haven't quite scratched the surface. But I want you to commit to this, because it is not going to be easy. It will be worth it in the end, that I truly believe. So can you agree to commit to therapy, which is really a commitment to yourself?"

Melissa bit at a hangnail that started to bleed. She shoved her hand into a pocket, not wanting to bleed on the pillow or couch. Dr. David handed her a tissue, which she took. "I don't want to be alone, and I don't want to hurt people. I'd also like it if I could like myself again. I think I let Jeremy treat me the way he did because I thought I deserved it. I'd like to not deserve it."

"Melissa, you deserve love and kindness. I think I can help you discover that. So is this you committing?" Dr. David said firmly. Melissa had been rocking back and forth, clutching the pillow, trying to unconsciously self-soothe.

"Yes, I want that. God, why is that so hard for me to say?" Melissa asked as she gave in to needing a tissue. She wiped her face and blew her nose as Dr. David continued.

"Because denying parts of yourself and not allowing yourself to heal can make you believe you don't deserve inner peace. I have a feeling you've been waging an internal war with yourself for longer than you'd care to admit." Dr. David gave her a kind smile. "I'm really glad you're here and ready to work."

The rest of the session was mostly Melissa crying, but through the snot and tears, spilling her mental guts all over Dr. David's office. To his credit, he stayed professional through her explaining the breakup and the revenge plot. He didn't diagnose her, even though part of Melissa craved being told what was wrong with her and prayed there was a magic pill that could make her normal. He didn't, and no prescription was offered.

Melissa did feel like she'd unburdened herself quite a bit, but she still felt heavy, and after such a long emotional outburst, all she wanted to do was sleep. Before leaving, she booked a weekly appointment for the next six months. She wasn't sure if that was proof of her commitment or her admitting she was nuts. Still, the idea of weekly appointments gave her comfort, not just in routine but in the act of allowing her darkest thoughts to be aired out, no longer trapped in her mind.

Much like Dr. David had promised, every session was work. Melissa started journaling daily, reading books like *Lost Connections* by Johann Hari and *It's Not You* by

Ramani Durvasula, and refused to miss a single therapy session. After a few more sessions, Dr. David prescribed her a low dose of Lexapro. Things didn't instantly turn around and become perfect, but Melissa felt for the first time like they were heading toward positive progress. However, her bubble remained small, and she knew she had to apologize to five more people. Much like she remembered from before, she got what she gave in therapy. More effort inside therapy meant more results outside of it.

After a month, Melissa decided it was time to start her apology tour.

The first one was easy. Melissa took a small trip to Fool's Gold and found AKA Aloha. She apologized for throwing up and that she probably had to clean it up. Aloha barely remembered her, immediately accepted her apology if only to avoid prolonging the conversation, and took the bonus tip of one hundred dollars. Melissa really wasn't sure if that was enough or too much, but at the end of the day, it was what she could afford. Either way, Aloha was happy to have the money and Melissa felt relief.

Jenna and Brooke were two and three. She hadn't been nearly as horrible to them over the course of her revenge journey, but she acknowledged that her dip into insanity had affected them. So she invited them out to coffee without Sloan, not only to apologize but to thank them for being there for Sloan when she couldn't be. Jenna just wanted to suggest a lot of vitamins and essential oils to solve Melissa's mental state, and Brooke just wanted a promise that she wouldn't "pull that shit" again. She was pretty sure Sloan had pre smoothed the situation between the three of them, as they seemed very willing to forgive and move on. She wasn't going to look that gift horse in the mouth, so she agreed to breathe in more lavender oil and to not pull any shit ever again.

The fourth person was far more complicated and delicate. Logan. No matter if Logan never wanted to see her again after her apology, she knew that of all the victims of her insanity, he had been the most undeserving of it. Not that anyone deserved the way she treated them, but Logan had only wanted to get to know her. That had been his biggest crime. Somehow he'd been attracted to her, and she sucked him into a whirlpool of crazy.

Chapter 26: Where the Heart Is

Melissa walked into Stone's Throw Grocery, nerves spiking through her whole body. She knew interrupting him at work wasn't a great move, but showing up at his apartment would have been worse, and she worried that if she tried to call or text him, he would ignore her. Before he ignored her for the rest of time, she just needed him to know she was sorry.

She looked around and didn't see him at his normal counter, so she started walking the aisles until she saw him stocking cans. He didn't look like his usual carefree self, and guilt replaced her nerves. Had she broken him the way Jeremy had broken her? She forced herself to stay calm as she walked close enough not to look like she was creeping up on him before saying his name. His head snapped toward her in shock.

"Hey," Logan said, then looked back at the cans of corn he was stacking. Melissa wondered if he considered chucking one at her but knew he'd never physically hurt her. "I can't talk, I'm working."

"I screwed up, and you were right. I just wanted to tell you to your face that I'm sorry," Melissa blurted out. Logan didn't look at her but continued stocking cans.

"Careful, that sounded like someone in their right mind," Logan said. His tone was still stern, but hope sprang inside Melissa because at least he cracked a joke.

"I thought I'd try out sanity," Melissa said, hoping Logan could hear her sincerity.

"Wow, how's that feel?" Logan said, still stacking but occasionally glancing at her.

"Complicated. There was a certain rush with embracing the crazy," Melissa admitted. She could tell Logan wasn't a fan of that answer by how hard he set a can down, so she continued. "But I didn't like how it made my family or you feel. Rush or not, I wouldn't do it again."

"It really sucked having to tell my friends that you ditched me. Then having to explain that I brought the woman security was chasing out of the building," Logan said, picking up the empty box that once held cans. "Did you just use me? Like, was anything real? Because I keep trying to understand what happened. I know I helped you plan things, and maybe this is me being dumb, but I thought you liked me. I thought you'd drop that whole revenge thing, but you didn't."

"All I can say is I'm sorry and promise that I won't do that again. I have no idea how that particular event could happen, but I'm working through it in therapy. So I can promise that nothing similar or as grandiose is in my distant or near future plans," Melissa said, and while she meant every word, she couldn't help but feel like they rang hollow to Logan. "It's on me. I screwed everything up. You warned me before I went up there that I was going to hurt someone. It was me, which honestly was the best outcome, but I know I also hurt you. I don't know how to fix that. I'd do just about anything."

Logan started breaking down the box, deep in thought. He was mad at her and concerned for her. He was glad to hear she was making better choices, but was he willing to put his heart on the line for a woman freshly in therapy with a possible rap sheet? What would his friends say? His parents?

Melissa took his silence as an answer and reluctantly respected it. She knew he had every right to hate her forever. "I get it. I'll go. I'm sorry I did this here, I just really wanted to apologize to you face to face. I hope"

"I like pineapple on pizza," Logan blurted. The idea of never seeing Melissa again felt horrible, and if she was owning her issues and working on them, then that meant something. His friends and family would just have to get on board. "According to the internet, it's a red flag. I know you like knowing about my flaws. So what I have is no left pinky toe and pineapple on pizza are the best flaws I can offer. That and my aggressively average penis."

"Stop saying penis. We are in your parents' store," Melissa said as a smile crossed her face. Logan grabbed her hand and pulled her closer.

"Penis," he whispered before kissing her.

It was the kind of kiss that made other customers decide to skip buying canned goods but confirmed to Melissa and Logan that they were both on the same page for the first time since they'd met. Melissa only mildly regretted that their first kiss with her being sane started with penis, but Logan was already counting the minutes before he could brag to his friends that his rizz was so good that whispering penis led to a kiss.

After they finished kissing and made plans for dinner, Melissa made her way out of the store with customers giving her strange looks and, in the case of an eighty year old man, a wink. She knew now she had somehow managed to put her most important relationships back on track. She wouldn't be alone. She would have love. In her mind, that was a miracle.

However, AKA Aloha, Jenna, Brooke, and Logan were only four of the five people she was determined to make amends with. The fifth and final person who deserved an apology was going to take everything out of Melissa, because she knew she would have to swallow her pride and probably allow herself to be called Moppy again.

Rachel Moore.

Chapter 27: Mean Girls

It came as a real shock to Sloan when Melissa asked her to help set up a meeting. It took some convincing because Sloan was not sure of Melissa's true intentions, and part of her worried that Melissa was backsliding in her therapy process. After a week of begging, Sloan relented, trying desperately to hold onto the fact that Melissa had kept her promise about consistently going to therapy and that she had, of her own volition, made amends with Brooke and Jenna.

This request led Sloan on a journey of trying to create a bridge for the meeting without breaking a law or risking her license to practice law. With very few options, Sloan landed on going to Rachel Moore's office to ambush her when she arrived at work. Shockingly, Sloan's sudden appearance did not seem to rattle Rachel. She did not even seem to remember meeting Sloan until she brought up Melissa. While Rachel was not pleased by the prospect of seeing Melissa, she relented when Sloan promised that all Melissa wanted was to apologize and that the meeting would be at the Silver Slapjack at whatever time Rachel chose.

Sloan's reason for this ambush was that there would be no paper trail requesting the breaking of the restraining order. The day of, they would get there a full hour before the time Rachel chose. They would order food, pretend a third person was not coming, and act like they were simply having a girls' day. Melissa had agreed to never admit to or say aloud anything that could be used in court against her. These were Sloan's nonnegotiables for setting this up.

On the two-month anniversary of Melissa's arrest and short-lived photography career, Melissa and Sloan sat at the Silver Slapjack. They ordered food and coffee, talked loudly about the baby, and, like Sloan had requested, pretended it was a simple girls' day. It did not stop Melissa from looking at the door so often that Sloan left a bruise on her shin from kicking her. Finally, after Melissa forced herself to finish a waffle, they spotted Rachel Moore entering the room. When she came in, Melissa felt all the hairs on her neck stand on end and worried her food might make a reappearance.

Sloan asked a nearby table for a chair for their surprise guest. Rachel arched her eyebrow suspiciously at the two women but sat down. If Melissa had to guess, she read right through Sloan's plausible deniability act but sat down regardless. Sloan kept a calm tone. "Would you like something to eat?"

"No," Rachel said, unimpressed with Sloan's opener.

Melissa found herself momentarily mute. Seeing Rachel like this was so odd. She no longer had a moral superiority or a victim card to play. She had not balanced karma's scales by trying to ruin Rachel's life, but in a way, Rachel had become the catalyst for Melissa's life to hit rock bottom and subsequently get back on course.

Rachel's annoyance with the silence reached a fever pitch. "I'm waiting to hear something the police haven't told me."

"I thought I'd say something really inspired when I saw you, but it's as simple as this. I was in a really bad place. I was not thinking clearly. I am truly horrified that I allowed myself to spiral as much as I did, and I am sincerely sorry for any pain, suffering, trauma, or anything negative I caused. I promise I will never contact you again. I just wanted to say it directly to you. That I know I screwed up and I deeply regret it."

"What, no 'blah blah I tormented you and that's why I went psycho on you' BS?" Rachel asked, lips pursed and eyes narrowed.

Melissa took a deep breath and weighed her thoughts. "I think you know what you did, what happened when we were kids. I'm only starting to understand why, but I did this as an adult. I see now, after a few months of therapy, that what I did is far worse."

Sloan reached her hand under the table and held it.

"Damn right, Melissa. I was a little shit as a kid. Granted, I'm still a bitch as an adult. I own that. I know who I am. It serves me and what I do, and gives me the life I want." Rachel smirked, then looked at Melissa like she was doing a math problem in her head. Finally, she pulled an envelope from her Prada purse. "If you need a reason, I was bored as a kid, so I picked on you. You were sooo weak. A loser. I don't know why you. There were plenty of losers at that school, but you made it sooooo easy. So what? All this stupid nonvictim victimhood nonsense. You said it. You're an adult. Get over it."

"I'm working on it. Again, I am sorry for any emotional." Melissa said quickly.

The hand holding under the table shifted from Sloan comforting Melissa to Melissa signaling for Sloan to stay quiet as Sloan's outrage over Rachel's rationale for bullying began to seep into her body language. Rachel clearly enjoyed Sloan's discomfort.

"Eh, gross. Emotional damage? Oh, poor me? Fuck right off," Rachel said, rolling her eyes, then suddenly pushed the envelope toward Melissa. "We are square. You hear me? It's the number of a woman I was going to send to you before the hotel incident."

"I'm not into women, but thanks." Melissa began, confused by the gesture.

Rachel cut her off, annoyed by her lack of comprehension. "Could've fooled me, Mel. Ugh, Mel. Terrible name. Your mom must not have liked you much." Unable to resist the insult, she continued, "It's for a job. Same level as your last position with room to grow. I even negotiated a better salary. You're welcome."

Melissa looked down at the envelope, then back at Rachel, a whirl of gratitude, shock, and relief hitting her at once. If this was real, her life could stop being at a standstill. She could move forward. She forced the tears welling in her eyes back because she knew Rachel would see them as weakness. "That is really kind. Thank you."

"I'm not the model of feminism most people think of. Whatever. I believe women should help women in business." For a moment, a flash of humanity crossed her face, then disappeared just as quickly. "Lose my number. Have a life."

Melissa stood at the same time as Rachel and offered her hand. They shook. Melissa was not sure why she had done it, but it felt like they had played a long game of chess. A game Rachel did not even know she had been playing, and yet somehow, she still won.

"Goodbye, Rachel Moore," Melissa said as she watched her leave, her thoughts still spinning. Rachel had been her greatest enemy in her mind. She had been the Tonya Harding to her Nancy Kerrigan, but in the end, they had swapped roles.

"Are you doing alright?" Sloan asked, then suddenly gripped Melissa's hand painfully tight.

"I mean, I suppose. Are you?" Melissa asked.

"No. I think you should get the car. I need to leave a really big tip," Sloan said, making a strange face.

Melissa gave her a puzzled look. Sloan continued, "My water broke. We should go."

"Call Zach and tell him to meet us at the hospital. I'll be right back," Melissa said, springing toward the door.

Despite the intensity of finding out the baby was coming, Melissa felt a rush of excitement and lightness. She pulled the car to the front of the restaurant. Sloan had managed to waddle outside and was leaning on a half wall that divided the outdoor diners from the sidewalk. Melissa ran to open the door for her as Sloan moved slowly toward the seat.

"There is a towel in the trunk. Could you put it on my seat? My pants are wet," Sloan said pragmatically, with no shame.

Melissa nodded and rushed to the trunk. As she flung it open, she heard a familiar voice call her name. She turned to see Jeremy wearing a baby Bjorn and a running suit. Shock froze her in place. Aside from some bags under his eyes, he looked the same as the last time she saw him.

"It's been a minute. Meet little Jeremy Junior, or as we call him, JJ," he said, lifting one of JJ's chunky arms to make him wave at Melissa, who forced a polite smile.

"This fucking guy," Sloan muttered to herself. Normally she would have been wittier or stepped in to help Melissa, but a contraction flooded her brain with pain.

Melissa looked at JJ, and for a dark moment, thought about how that could have been her son. For the first time, though, the thought was not sad but horrifying. In another life, she would have been saddled to this terrible man.

"Wow, he's cute. Congrats," Melissa said as she grabbed the towel and closed the trunk. She felt bad, but she did not think JJ was that cute, and the abbreviation of his name made him sound like a sleazy salesman. With a dad like Jeremy, that did not seem unlikely.

Melissa tried to move past Jeremy to get to Sloan, but he blocked her. "Wow, so you don't even ask about me? Or my kid? Nothing?"

"What? I owe you nothing. You made it clear I was nothing to you. Why should I ask about you?" Melissa said, pushing past him and placing the towel on the front passenger seat. "Sloan needs me. She's in labor. You obviously don't, because you left me, and I certainly don't need you."

"Hell yes, Mel. Fuck you, pencil dick," Sloan said as she began to squat, with Melissa's help.

"Don't worry about him. We need to go," Melissa said calmly.

Jeremy bristled. "You know, Melissa, you're a bitch, and Sloan, you've always been a massive cun-"

In a sudden burst of herculean strength, Sloan pushed herself upright and lunged forward, sucker punching Jeremy square in the face. "What the fuck? I'm holding a baby, you nut job!"

"Sloan, car, now," Melissa said, forcing and helping Sloan into the passenger seat.

Jeremy's face was gushing blood. Sloan had hit him straight on the nose.

"I'm holding a baby, you psycho," he screamed.

"I'm birthing one, bitch," Sloan shouted as the door slammed shut.

Jeremy tilted his head back, trying to stop the bleeding, but blood had already gone everywhere, including the top of JJ's head. JJ blew spit bubbles, seemingly unfazed by the chaos surrounding his father.

Melissa flipped Jeremy off triumphantly as she walked around to the driver's side. Before getting in, she took one last look at him and borrowed a line from Rachel.

"Have a life, Jeremy," she said with a smile.

Her joy was not at Jeremy's pain, but at the fact that she never would have imagined this would be the closure she got. She was, in fact, in the process of having a life, a really happy one if she continued down her current path. Jeremy would never apologize or realize how he had hurt her. Even if he did, she doubted he would care. What mattered more was that she no longer needed it from him. Melissa could move on.

"I told you to have your shit together by the time the baby came. You really got there just under the wire," Sloan said, doing her calming Lamaze breaths.

Melissa laughed. She had thought the same thing. She had just finished her apology tour, landed a job lead, and even squeezed in telling Jeremy off. She had kept her promise to Sloan before the baby came.

"I can't believe you punched him," Melissa said through laughter.

"And it felt so good," Sloan said, then gripped the car's handlebar as another contraction ripped through her.

Melissa glanced at the GPS guiding them to the hospital. "Hang in there, lady. Five minutes and we'll be there," she said, hoping her tone sounded soothing and not panicked.

"I'm so proud of you, Mel. Like, for real. You owned your shit, and you're you again. Just in time for this thing," Sloan said, pointing at her belly.

"You may want to not call your baby a thing. Could give it a complex," Melissa said, half deflecting the compliment.

"Don't you start calling my baby it, then," Sloan joked.

"I couldn't have gotten here if you hadn't told me the truth at your shower and then shown up for me at the police station. You've always been there for me," Melissa said, unable to stop the sappiness from creeping into her voice.

"You're my girl," Sloan said, patting Melissa's arm, then grabbing it viciously.

"You're my girl too," Melissa said, trying to breathe through the pain radiating up her arm as she became Sloan's new squeeze toy. "You're going to be a mom. Holy shit."

Melissa spotted the hospital ER drop off zone and even saw Zach pacing by the entrance. When the car pulled up, Zach swung the door open and rushed a wheelchair over for Sloan. Sloan could tell he was about to say something that would annoy her, so she cut him off.

"I don't want to hear it. I wanted to be there. I thought they were Braxton Hicks. I regret nothing," Sloan said with every ounce of sass she could muster, then turned to Melissa. "Park the car and get your ass up there."

"I'll be there," Melissa said, pulling away to park.

Chapter 28: Nine Months

The rest of the day felt like a blur for Melissa, Zach, and Sloan. Melissa remembered panic coursing through her veins as she found Sloan and Zach in the birthing suite. Zach looked on the brink of passing out or throwing up from fear and excitement but was determined to be a rock for Sloan. Sloan had many feelings in that moment. While some were positive, the loudest one was, "If someone doesn't get this baby out of me, I will give myself a C-section."

Apparently, Sloan's contractions were extremely close together, and the kid was ready to vacate the womb. She had woken up that morning feeling contractions but convinced herself they were Braxton Hicks and ignored them. So when Zach got her call, he was filled with righteous outrage at being right, followed immediately by panic because she was not with him. He refused to leave her side, holding her hand in the hospital room, and before words could be exchanged, Melissa was handed Sloan's right leg.

Sloan and Melissa had been close for a long time. They had seen each other in various states of undress, from quick changes to sharing hotel rooms on trips. But neither had seen the other's vagina, let alone the inner workings. After Melissa was handed Sloan's leg, she could no longer say that. She saw everything, and stranger still, a baby was coming out of it. If you are not a medical professional, which Melissa certainly was not, the view was briefly shell-shocking.

"Oh my god, is that the head?" Melissa remembered asking, and while her question was confirmed by the doctor, the birth itself felt like both a million years and two seconds at once. She later rationalized that time simply loses meaning in moments like that. Sloan would later confirm that birth felt like being ripped in two and that she had broken her tailbone from pushing. Essentially, birth is a battlefield of blood, feces, and trauma that is then forgotten the moment the baby is placed in the parents' arms.

After the doctor confirmed the baby was fine and the afterbirth was delivered, she said a quick goodbye and rushed off to deliver another baby in a different room. Nurses continued to fuss, take measurements, and clean the aftermath while the baby cried. Melissa was torn between watching this new life and watching her friend. Sloan looked like a statue, unblinking and unmoving, tracking every nurse's movement. Zach hovered near them at Sloan's direction.

Officially, Rowan Melvin Wolfe was born at 12:30 p.m., roughly two hours after Sloan walked through the hospital doors. He weighed a solid eight pounds, one ounce and measured twenty-one inches long, the picture of health. Melissa was the fourth person to hold him, after the doctor and his parents. He was a squishy, soft bundle of love with lungs so powerful Melissa wondered if he would grow up to be a theater kid like his dad. She made a silent vow to be the best auntie she could.

After a few more minutes of ogling Rowan and showering Sloan with praise, Melissa excused herself. She wanted Zach and Sloan to have alone time with their new family, and she also selfishly wanted a quiet moment to herself. The day had been so much in the best possible way.

Melissa had achieved her original goal, in a way. She had made things right for herself by accepting responsibility for her actions and standing up for herself. More than that, though, she had so much to look forward to with the people around her. Sloan was a mom, which made Melissa an auntie. She could already picture being the fun aunt, sneaking him treats, showing him the best books, and hopefully avoiding teaching him his first swear word.

She still had Logan, somehow. He had forgiven her and fully supported her therapy journey. He loved her so much that she sometimes wondered if he also needed therapy, but he always felt like a sea of green flags. It shut off the logic in her brain and allowed whimsy to take over, so much so that she agreed to let him teach her how to play DnD. As long as she got to be near him, it sounded like a pretty sweet deal, even if playing a fantasy elf was not her usual vibe.

He was the first person she texted while walking to Sloan's car. She planned to drive it back to their house since Zach's car was the one with the baby seat installed. Logan had agreed to meet her there and then take her to her mom's place. She had not told him yet, but she was planning to introduce him to Cheryl. She was certain the only thing he would worry about was not having time to buy Cheryl a gift or flowers.

As Melissa sat in the car smiling at both her near and distant future, she realized tears were sliding down her face. For the first time in as long as she could remember, she was genuinely excited about her future and even her present. She laughed at herself, wiped the tears away, and started the engine.

In the words of Rachel Moore, Melissa was ready to have a life.

Pop Culture Appendix

Thank you for reading this labor of love. As you probably picked up on the many pop culture references throughout the book, you may be wondering why. Because I couldn't help myself and it's my book. If television writers can name episodes after songs, why not name chapters after movies? So here is a breakdown of some of the movies, songs, and other media directly mentioned. Hopefully, this will help you through the slump of finishing a book.

Chapters

Each chapter is named after a movie I've watched and in some way connected to the chapter itself. Some of these movies are classics, personal guilty pleasures, and even a few I only saw once but whose scenes live forever in my mind rent-free. The scores are based on Rotten Tomatoes.

★ Office Space (1999) Comedy - Score 81%

★ He's Just Not That Into You (2009) Comedy - Score 41%

★ Mamma Mia! (2008) Musical Comedy - Score 55%

★ The Money Pit (1986) Comedy - Score 50%

★ New Moon (2009) Romance - Score 28%

★ The Breakfast Club (1985) Comedy - Score 89%

★ Eighth Grade (2018) Comedy - Score 99%

★ Little Miss Sunshine (2006) Comedy - Score 91%

★ Life of the Party (2018) Comedy - Score 38%

★ Bombshell (2019) Thriller - Score 68%

★ Trainwreck (2015) Comedy - Score 84%

★ Date Night (2010) Comedy - Score 67%

- ★ Clueless (1995) Comedy - Score 81%
- ★ Booksmart (2019) Comedy - Score 96%
- ★ Knives Out (2019) Mystery - Score 92%
- ★ The Devil Wears Prada (2006) Comedy - Score 75%
- ★ Fool's Gold (2008) Comedy - Score 11%
- ★ The Gentlemen (2019) Comedy - Score 75%
- ★ Inside Out (2015) Comedy - Score 98%
- ★ Baby Mama (2008) Comedy - Score 63%
- ★ Employee of the Month (2006) Comedy - Score 20%
- ★ The Wedding Date (2005) Comedy - Score 11%
- ★ It's Complicated (2009) Comedy - Score 59%
- ★ Legally Blonde (2001) Comedy - Score 71%
- ★ Silver Linings Playbook (2012) Comedy - Score 92%
- ★ Where the Heart Is (2000) Romance - Score 35%
- ★ Mean Girls (2004) Comedy - Score 84%
- ★ Nine Months (1995) Comedy - Score 27%

Other Movies and Television Shows Mentioned

- ★ Saved! (2004) Comedy - Score 61%
- ★ The Princess Diaries (2001) Comedy - Score 49%
- ★ Supernatural (2005 to 2020) Drama - Score 93%
- ★ Gilmore Girls (2000 to 2007) Drama - Score 88%
- ★ Yellowstone (2018 to present) Drama - Score 84%

Bands and Songs Mentioned

- ★ Cry Me a River by Justin Timberlake
- ★ Sweet but Psycho by Ava Max

- ★ SOS by Rihanna

- ★ Giants in the Sky from Into the Woods

- ★ Adele

- ★ Alanis Morissette

- ★ Bon Jovi

- ★ Paramore

- ★ Panic! At the Disco

- ★ Taylor Swift

- ★ Britney Spears

- ★ Miley Cyrus

Books and Scripts Mentioned

- ★ Hamlet by William Shakespeare (1602)

- ★ Heathers The Musical by Kevin Murphy and Laurence O'Keefe (2010)

- ★ Lost Connections by Johann Hari (2018)

- ★ It's Not You by Ramani Durvasula (2024) Also has a fascinating YouTube channel!

Podcasts Mentioned

- ★ Buried Bones with Kate Winkler Dawson and Paul Holes

Hopefully you loved this book or at the very least walked away with a list of recommended movies, shows, books, and even a podcast.